'Why bother to kiss me at all?'

'I'm a scientist. I wanted to know whether you were telling the truth.'

'So that *mauling* I just suffered was by way of being an *experiment*?'

'A very effective one, you must admit,' Drew said in a maddeningly reasonable tone.

'I wouldn't describe it like that.'

'Come on, Carey, why not face the truth for once? Your mouth said one thing but your body gave me quite a different answer!'

Dear Reader

It's the time of year when nights are long and cold, and there's nothing better than relaxing with a Mills & Boon story! To help you banish those winter blues, we've got some real treats in store for you this month. Enjoy the first book in our exciting new LOVE LETTERS series, or forget the weather outside and lose yourself in one of our exotic locations. It's almost as good as a real winter holiday!

The Editor

Jessica Hart had a haphazard career before she began writing to finance a degree in history. Her experience ranged from waitress, theatre production assistant and outback cook to newsdesk secretary, expedition PA and English teacher, and she has worked in countries as different as France and Indonesia, Australia and Cameroon. She now lives in the North of England, where her hobbies are limited to eating and drinking and travelling when she can, preferably to places where she'll find good food or desert or tropical rain.

Recent titles by the same author:

LOVE'S LABYRINTH
THE RIGHT KIND OF MAN

MOONSHADOW MAN

BY
JESSICA HART

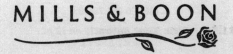

MILLS & BOON

MILLS & BOON LIMITED
ETON HOUSE, 18-24 PARADISE ROAD
RICHMOND, SURREY TW9 1SR

*MILLS & BOON and the Rose Device
are trademarks of the publisher.*

*First published in Great Britain 1994
by Mills & Boon Limited*

© Jessica Hart 1994

*Australian copyright 1994   Philippine copyright 1995
This edition 1995*

ISBN 0 263 78818 0

*Set in Times Roman 10 on 12 pt.
01-9501-55474 C*

Made and printed in Great Britain

CHAPTER ONE

DREW TARRANT wasn't what Carey was expecting at all.

'You don't need to worry about the marine biologists,' Camilla had assured her gaily. 'You know how vague scientists are. They'll be so wrapped up in their fish, they probably won't even notice you're there at all.'

But there was nothing vague about Drew Tarrant. He was a tall, lean, very compact man with dark brown hair and a pair of cool, watchful green eyes that were startlingly light against his tan. Carey's first impression was of a controlled, incisive power that was somehow only increased by the fact that he wore a pair of obviously old cotton trousers and a faded khaki shirt with the sleeves rolled casually up to the elbows.

'Camilla Cavendish?' His voice was crisp, his expression uncomfortably acute and so penetrating that Carey had to force herself not to flinch. He looked her up and down, and it was as if he could see right through her and had already labelled her a liar and an imposter.

How had he guessed so quickly? she wondered wildly. One look into those piercing eyes was enough to convince her that she would never get away with this charade Camilla had forced her into. Carey stood in the airport and wished fervently that she had never heard of Belize or Moonshadow Cay and that she was safely back home in Yorkshire instead of trying to dupe this unnerving man with his sharp, intelligent eyes. It was hard to imagine anyone who looked *less* easy to fool. She would never get away with it.

Every instinct told her to turn round and jump smartly back on to the plane, but the memory of its hair-raisingly bumpy descent through the black storm clouds was enough to make her hesitate. Could Drew Tarrant really be intimidating enough to force her back on to a plane which appeared to be flown by a suicidally lunatic pilot? He might not look very friendly, but at least he wasn't dangerous; she was bound to be safer with two feet firmly on the ground.

Drew was watching her impatiently, but there was no suspicion in his eyes and cool reason came flooding back. He couldn't possibly know that she wasn't Camilla. Besides, she couldn't turn tail and run. She was here now, and she would have to see it through. She had promised Camilla.

Sinkingly aware that this was the point of no return, Carey took a deep breath and looked Drew Tarrant squarely in the eye. 'Yes,' she said. 'I'm Camilla.'

'Absolutely not!' Carey had said firmly when Camilla had first broached the idea.

'But Carey, you've got to help me,' wailed her cousin. 'You've just been saying how much you wanted to get away for a while.'

'Camilla, when I talk about getting away, I mean a week in the Lake District. I don't mean some mosquito-ridden island off the coast of a country I hadn't even heard of before you arrived.'

'Only you could describe a tropical island as *mosquito-ridden*,' said Camilla with a sigh. 'Honestly, most girls would jump at the chance of a free fortnight in the Caribbean! I've seen some photos and it looks fabulous: palm trees, white sand, blue lagoons...you'll love it.'

'I get bored lying on a beach all day,' Carey pointed out. 'I'd rather go for a good walk, and I don't fancy two weeks walking round and round in circles, which is all I'd be able to do if this island is as small as you say it is.'

Camilla eyed her cousin with exasperated affection. The two girls were having tea in front of a blazing fire in Carey's Yorkshire cottage. Camilla was lying on the sofa, her right leg, encased in plaster up to the knee, propped up on some cushions, while Carey sat cross-legged and straight-backed on the floor. She was a calmly practical girl with wide, humorous grey eyes and rather ordinary brown hair that hung straight to her shoulders. Today she had pulled it away from her face with a thin black ribbon, emphasising her beautiful bone-structure and the fine, glowing skin. Carey was the first person to admit that her looks weren't striking, but there was a quiet charm about her that lingered in the memory and effectively disguised a surprisingly stubborn personality and a sense of humour that Camilla privately considered uncomfortably astringent at times.

The cousins had been close ever since the yearly summer holidays had been spent together as children and they had remained good friends in spite of or perhaps because of the differences in their characters. Where Carey was cool and sensible, Camilla was flamboyant. Carey was a country girl, Camilla was relentlessly ambitious and fond of claiming that she wouldn't be seen dead in a pair of gumboots. She was beautiful, glamorous, un-ashamedly seductive and could be utterly ruthless when it came to getting her own way.

She was thinking of how to persuade Carey to go along with her plan now as she sipped her tea. 'It would only be for two weeks...oh, *please*, Carey, won't you do it for me?' she wheedled, resorting to what Carey later pointed out was nothing less than emotional blackmail. 'Look at all the times I covered up for you when we were little! I pulled you out of that river and spent all night helping you look for that stupid dog of yours and I never told your mother about you and Phil, did I? Why, I even gave you one of my dolls when you left yours on the train, and *now*, when I need you to help me out on something really important, you won't even consider it!'

Carey buttered a crumpet. She knew perfectly well how unscrupulous Camilla could be, but there was a strong bond between them. Her cousin had a much warmer heart than most people gave her credit for. She hid it well behind her image of glossy sophistication, but she had always stood up for her quieter cousin, and when Carey's mother had died the previous year it had been Camilla who had been there for her.

'I don't understand why you want *me* to go,' she said rather indistinctly as she took a bite of the crumpet. 'Wouldn't it be better to send someone from your company?'

'That's the last thing I want!' Camilla sat up with a grimace and shoved another cushion behind her back, shaking her hair away from her face. It was naturally brown, like Carey's, but cleverly highlighted so that it glimmered gold in the light from the lamp behind her. 'Look, I'll have to start at the beginning so that you can see how important this is to me. You remember I started work for Weatherill Willis six months ago?'

Carey licked the butter from her fingers and nodded. Weatherill Willis was a well-known firm of property developers specialising in exotic and luxurious developments.

'I'm in PR at the moment,' Camilla explained, 'but what I really want to do is to become one of the executives who come up with the initial ideas. They're the people who spot the potential in a place no one's ever thought of before. They rely on contacts a lot, but they do a lot of travelling as well, deciding which sites are worth developing.'

'That sounds more like a permanent holiday than a job,' commented Carey with a gleam of humour as she poured herself another cup of tea.

Camilla bristled, as Carey had known she would. 'It's not nearly as easy as it sounds,' she said importantly. 'You've got to have real flair, and it's terribly hard to get into... but I think I've found a way!' The dramatic pause was typical of Camilla, Carey thought, watching over the rim of her teacup as her cousin leant forward persuasively. 'I met a man called Emory Jones at a party a few weeks ago. He told me that he was from Belize. I knew it was in Central America somewhere, but what I didn't know was that it's got one of the longest coral reefs in the world. Apparently its a fantastic place for diving and snorkelling, and, best of all, it's completely unspoilt.'

Camilla glanced at Carey to see how she was reacting, but she could be infuriatingly inscrutable at times. Suppressing a sigh, Camilla persevered with her description. 'Inside the reef are hundreds of little islands they call cays—they're spelt like bays but pronounced "keys"—most of them undeveloped, uninhabited and perfect places to get away from it all. Emory owns a tiny island called Moonshadow Cay, which he's thinking about developing if he could get some investment. He showed me some photos, Carey, and as soon as I saw them I knew this was my big chance to show that I had the flair and instincts to spot development sites as well. Apparently there are a couple of high-powered marine scientists working on some research project there, but apart from them the cay is completely deserted. It would make the most beautiful resort, Carey. People will pay anything to go somewhere different and we'd make it very up-market and exclusive, of course.'

'Of course,' Carey echoed drily.

Camilla shot her a suspicious look. Carey had some odd ideas sometimes, and Camilla was never quite sure whether her cousin was making fun of her or not. She decided to ignore it and continue with her story. 'I decided to go straight to the top, so I took the photographs to the senior partner and asked if I could go and look at the island for myself and see what potential it really had for development, or if Emory had missed some eyesore out of the pictures. I could see Josh was impressed,' she told Carey, preening herself at the memory. 'And then I had a stroke of luck, because he said the name Moonshadow Cay rang a sort of bell with him. It turns out that Weatherill Willis is sponsoring part of the project those marine biologists are working on, so the least they can do in return for all the money we're giving them is look after me while I'm there. The project leader's called Dr Tarrant. Apparently he's quite well-known. Did you ever see a television series called *Beneath the Blue*? It was some natural history programme about marine life.'

Carey thought, then shook her head. 'I don't think so.'

'Well, apparently this Drew Tarrant wrote and presented it,' Camilla told her. 'I didn't see it either, but I've heard that it was fantastic. A friend of mine used to watch it every week. She said he was gorgeous!' She glanced regretfully down at her plaster. 'I was looking forward to meeting him! A beautiful coral island *and* a gorgeous man...I might have known it was too good to be true,' she said wistfully. 'Everything was perfect. I'd sent a message explaining the situation and telling him when I was arriving. The ticket was fixed up. All I had to do was go and bring back an idea that would give me a real foothold in the firm...and then I had to go skiing and break my stupid ankle!'

'I can see that it's disappointing,' said Carey, 'but I still don't see why it has to be me. Why can't you ask one of your colleagues to go in your place?'

'What, and let them pinch my idea?' cried Camilla, horrified. 'You've no idea what it's like, Carey! The competition to get ahead is cut-throat and there's no way anyone would go out to Belize, do my research for me and tamely hand it over to me when they got home. Suddenly it would be all their idea. No, it has to be you, Carey,' she finished passionately. 'You're the only one I can trust!'

Carey's grey eyes twinkled appreciatively. 'I'd no idea I had such a melodramatic role to play!'

'You can mock, but it's true,' Camilla insisted with a sulky look. 'It's all right for you, running your nice little gift shop in your nice little town, but where I work it's the survival of the fittest!' Biting her lip, she slid a sideways look at Carey. 'I can't afford to lose this chance, Carey,' she pleaded. 'There's no way I can go swanning off to a coral reef with my leg in plaster, but there's nothing to stop you going.'

'Only a shop to run,' Carey pointed out with a crisp edge to her voice. 'It might not be a high-powered career, but it's all I've got. I can't just drop everything to jaunt off to the Caribbean!'

'I've thought of that,' said Camilla triumphantly. 'I can't stay in London in case someone sees me when they know I'm supposed to be in Belize, so while you're away I'll come up here and keep an eye on things for you. A broken ankle won't stop me sitting in your shop and stirring up a bit of trade. You can't tell me things are that busy in February, anyway?'

'Well, no,' admitted Carey reluctantly. She had the nasty feeling that she was being boxed into a corner. 'It's just...well, it's a crazy idea! I can't possibly pretend to be you.'

'Of course you can. Nobody in Belize is going to know who I am. Who's going to know that you're not me?'

'What about this supposedly gorgeous scientist, for a start?'

'They're expecting a Miss C. Cavendish, you *are* Miss C. Cavendish, and if they insist you can show your passport to prove it. Not that you'll need to,' Camilla went on after a moment's reflection. 'I went out with a marine biologist once. He was rather sweet, but completely vague. Terribly clever, of course, but he didn't know what day of the week it was half the time. I'll bet you anything these two are the same.'

'This Dr Tarrant or whatever his name is can't be that vague if he's presented a whole series on television,' Carey pointed out sceptically, but Camilla waved her doubts away.

'Oh, he'll know his stuff all right, but when it comes to day-to-day practicalities he probably won't have a clue. They'll both be so wrapped up in their fish, you'll be lucky if they notice you at all. We'll just have to hope they're on the ball enough to remember to pick you up from the airport!'

'I hope they're not that absent-minded if I have to rely on them for two weeks!' Too late, Carey heard the agreement implicit in her words and she sighed as Camilla beamed at her.

'I *knew* you'd help me out!'

'You haven't told me what I'm supposed to do with myself for two weeks,' Carey reminded her hastily, doing her best to backtrack.

'I want you to be my pair of eyes. Take a good hard look at the island: how long does it take to get there, what the swimming's like, are there clouds of mosquitoes everywhere... that kind of thing. You need to be able to give me as good an idea of the cay as if I'd been there myself, because I'll have to persuade the partners that I know exactly what the situation is. And take lots of photographs. You're a brilliant photographer, Carey, and your pictures could sell the whole project. Who knows? It might be a break for you too. You've been going on about giving up the shop to become a full-time photographer; now here's your chance to do a really professional job *and* live on a deserted island.' Camilla sent her cousin a cajoling smile. 'Come on, Carey! Where's your sense of adventure and romance?'

Carey grimaced. 'I've had enough of romance recently, thank you!' she retorted, but Camilla merely waved a disparaging hand.

'Giles doesn't count as romance. I don't know how you stuck with him for so long. He's so dull and respectable.'

'He's not dull,' Carey defended him a little half-heartedly. 'He's very nice.'

'So nice that he turns round and gets engaged to another girl five minutes after you've said no and now refuses to talk to you at all?'

'OK, so I was a bit hurt,' Carey admitted, sounding uncharacteristically defensive. 'But he did ask me to marry him and I refused, so I can't blame him for finding someone else. I just wish he'd stop treating me as if I were some kind of traitor. It makes things very awkward in a small town.'

Camilla leant across and put her cup down on the coffee-table. 'If you ask me, my offer couldn't have been better timed,' she said complacently. 'You're in a rut, Carey. You've been stuck in the same place for years, carrying on with the shop for your mother's sake, seeing the same old people, going out with boring old Giles, being sensible and safe, but if that's what you *really* wanted you'd have married him when he asked you to, wouldn't you?'

'I thought it *was* what I wanted for a long time,' Carey remembered a little sadly. 'But when it came down to it, I knew I couldn't marry him. I suppose if I was honest I'd just admit that I've still got an old-fashioned dream of meeting someone perfect,' she said with a rather shamefaced laugh. 'And Giles just wasn't.' She grimaced. 'Sometimes I wonder if the perfect man even exists.'

'Well, if he does, you're certainly not going to meet him sitting here in your cottage,' said Camilla practically. 'You need to get out and do something completely different...and what could be more different from Yorkshire in February than a Caribbean island?'

Carey sighed and stared into the fire. Camilla was right. She had been feeling restless recently...but *Belize*? 'You don't think the whole idea's a bit...well, dishonest?'

'No,' said Camilla, not even considering the matter. 'Really, Carey, you're so Puritan sometimes! It's not as if you're going to take advantage of anyone, is it? The only people you're likely to meet are the two scientists, and it won't make any difference to them which Miss Cavendish they get. But it *will* make a difference to me.' She looked at Carey who was chewing her cheek indecisively. 'Oh, Carey, *please* say you'll do it!'

Carey gave in. 'All right,' she said, and grinned as a radiant smile spread over Camilla's face. 'I just hope it's not another of your good ideas that I'll live to regret!'

'It won't be,' said Camilla positively. 'This trip is going to change your life, just you wait and see!'

Less than a week later, Carey was staring into Drew Tarrant's green eyes and wondering what madness had possessed her to agree to such a crazy scheme. The trip might well change her life, but all the present indications were that it wasn't going to be for the better. Camilla had insisted that she wear one of her suits to arrive in, claiming that she might as well try and create a suitably businesslike impression. The cream linen skirt and jacket were flattering, but Carey felt ill at ease in such unfamiliar sophistication, and it was obvious that Drew Tarrant was totally unimpressed.

She smiled a little nervously as she acknowledged his greeting, but her smile was not returned. For an instant, he looked taken aback, but the surprise vanished almost immediately as the keen, cool appraisal in his eyes darkened with contempt and an unmistakable hostility that left Carey bewildered and more than a little shaken.

Drew picked up her suitcase without another word and strode towards the exit, leaving Carey to trail after him. However he had managed to get his own television series, it certainly hadn't been through charm, she reflected. It was hard to imagine him relaxed and smiling in front of the camera. What was it Camilla's friend had claimed? That she wasn't the slightest bit interested in marine ecology, but had watched every programme in the series just to sigh over the gorgeous presenter? Carey looked at Drew's straight back marching ahead of her and sniffed. Gorgeous was not the word *she* would have chosen to describe him!

Outside, it was raining. Carey was used to rain in Yorkshire, of course, but she had never seen anything quite like this before. Here in the tropics the air was hot and clammy and the rain pounded down in an impenetrable curtain, crashing on to the roof of the terminal and splattering into great puddles in the car park. So much for the sunny paradise Camilla had promised her!

Carey hesitated by the door, awed in spite of herself by the rain's ferocity, and unprepared for the way the heat seemed to wrap itself around her like a suffocating blanket. She waited for Drew to suggest that they wait until the rain had eased off, but the idea didn't seem to have occurred to him.

'We'll have to run for it,' he said briefly, and set off across the car park.

Carey stared crossly after his rapidly retreating figure. He might at least have offered to bring the car round to her. He hadn't so much as glanced round to see whether she was following or not!

Suppressing a sigh, Carey bent to pick up her bag once more and stepped gingerly out into the rain. She was drenched within seconds, and the linen skirt clung uncomfortably to her legs, making it difficult to run. Drew seemed to have parked the car as far away from the terminal as possible; by the time she reached it, breathless and sodden and holding on to her temper with difficulty, Carey was sure he had done it deliberately.

He reached across and opened the passenger door, and Carey half scrambled, half fell inside, shaking the rain from her hands and leaning forward to squeeze the worst of the wet from her hair before any more could run down her neck. Still breathing heavily, she sat back in her seat and turned to find Drew watching her, his eyes alight with malicious amusement, and the shadow of a smile around his mouth. Unprepared for the way it transformed his expression, Carey froze in the middle of wiping the rain from her cheeks with the heel of her palm, resenting his obvious enjoyment of her own transformation from sophisticated businesswoman to bedraggled waif, but unable somehow to look away. His eyes, so cool, so piercing, held her immobile and all she could do was stare helplessly back at him.

The faded shirt stuck damply across his broad shoulders and the dark hair was plastered to his head, but he managed to look crisp and self-possessed and alarmingly tough, while she simply felt wet. The rain thundered on the metal roof of the car, but to Carey it seemed to her as if the noise faded, leaving them isolated in a bubble of silence, cut off from the outside world by the rain.

She was never sure how long they stared at each other, but slowly the amusement in those light eyes faded to be replaced by a dismaying mixture of puzzlement and distrust.

'So you're Camilla Cavendish,' said Drew slowly, and there was an odd note in his voice that Carey couldn't identify.

For some reason, her heart was lurching painfully against her ribs and it was difficult to breathe. Carey

told herself she was still breathless from her dash through
the rain and cleared her throat. 'Actually, I prefer to be
called Carey,' she said, managing to tear her eyes away
from his at last and hoping that she sounded more com-
posed than she felt.

'Carey?' Drew's expression sharpened with suspicion.
'Why?'

Why couldn't he just take her word for it? Carey wondered crossly. Perhaps she should have stuck to Camilla
after all, but she had had an obscure feeling that it was
important to keep as close to the truth as possible.
'Camilla's my first name,' she improvised wildly. 'But
I've always been called Carey at home. I just use Camilla
for business.'

'I was under the impression that you were here on
business,' said Drew sardonically. 'Or is this just a social
visit?'

'No, of course not.' Carey, still unsettled by the effect
of his eyes, was beginning to feel flustered. 'That is, I'm
here on business, but since we're going to be living
together on the island I just thought it would be more
pleasant if we were on informal terms.'

'Hmm.' Drew didn't sound very convinced. 'Carey?'
He seemed to be trying out the name, rolling it around
his mouth while he subjected her to an unnerving
scrutiny, the hard green gaze resting speculatively on her
clear grey eyes and the quiet intelligence in her face.
Carey swallowed and tucked her wet hair behind her ears
in an unconsciously nervous gesture, unaware of the way
it emphasised her pure bone-structure. 'Carey?' he said
again. 'It suits you better than Camilla.'

Carey wished he would stop looking at her like that.
Camilla always accused her of being infuriatingly calm
and unflappable, but she had never met anyone like Drew

Tarrant before. She had certainly never felt less calm. There was something about him that set her on edge. She wasn't sure whether it was the penetrating intelligence of his eyes or the air of suppressed hostility or simply the way his mouth curled intriguingly at one corner in direct contrast to the grim line of his brows which were pulled together over his nose in an increasingly suspicious stare. Irrelevantly, she wondered what he would look like when he smiled.

'Is something the matter?' she asked at last, her voice sharpened by unfamiliar nerves.

Drew continued to consider her thoughtfully. 'You're not what I was expecting,' he said.

'Oh?' Carey lifted her chin in unconscious defiance. 'And what exactly *were* you expecting?'

'Someone a lot more flamboyant,' he said slowly, without taking his eyes from her face. 'Someone smart, pushy, spoilt...more obviously glamorous, perhaps.'

Carey loved Camilla dearly, but she was far from blind to her faults. All too often her cousin came over precisely as Drew had described and she glanced at Drew uncertainly.

'I can see the description rings a bell, anyway,' he said sardonically, and an unexpected gleam of amusement sprang into Carey's grey eyes. He was more perceptive than he knew!

'Oh, it does,' she agreed demurely. 'It does indeed.'

Drew's frown deepened. He had seen the laughter in her eyes and it only seemed to make him more suspicious. 'I'm glad you find it so amusing,' he snapped. 'You might be very clever at hiding your true qualities behind that wide-eyed look, but you don't fool me. Your reputation precedes you, Miss Cavendish, so if you came here with the idea of pretending to be sweetly innocent you may as well give up now. You've picked the wrong man.'

The amusement vanished from Carey's eyes as she listened to him in astonishment and growing anger. 'I haven't got the faintest idea what you're talking about,' she said coldly. 'What do you mean by my "reputation"?'

'You thought we wouldn't know anything about you, didn't you?' he sneered. 'Well, I'm sorry to disappoint you, but I know all about you, Camilla Cavendish.'

'That seems highly unlikely, given that you met me for the first time a mere five minutes ago.' Carey had forgotten her nerves in fury. She wasn't prepared to sit here and listen to him insulting Camilla!

'I didn't need to meet you. I knew exactly what you were like before you arrived: a selfish, amoral, demanding, ambitious little tramp!'

'How dare you?' said Carey furiously. Her eyes blazed at him, and for a second surprise flared in his face as if he was taken aback by the force of her anger.

'Spare me the righteous indignation,' he said in a cutting tone. 'I'm not impressed.'

Carey struggled to keep her fury under control. 'Might I ask where you got this . . . this *slander* from?' she asked through clenched teeth. 'From someone who's met me for all of ten minutes, perhaps?'

'No,' said Drew icily. 'From someone who's had the misfortune to know you very well indeed.'

'Whoever it is obviously doesn't know me that well,' Carey retorted, her eyes still snapping dangerously. Camilla was no angel, but she certainly wasn't the monster Drew seemed determined to think her. 'If they did, they might have been able to describe me a little more accurately, and *you* might not have been so surprised when you came face to face with reality!' She eyed him with dislike. 'As a matter of fact, you weren't what *I* was expecting either, but I didn't insist on believing that I'd been right all along, in the face of all evidence to the contrary!'

Drew reached for the ignition key and switched on the engine. 'I'm sorry to disappoint you. No doubt you were expecting some gullible fool you could work your wiles on?'

'No,' said Carey frostily. 'I was expecting someone pleasant, courteous and welcoming. So I am disappointed, yes, but I doubt if you're very sorry!'

'Very perceptive of you!' There was a glint of humour in Drew's eyes as he turned to look over his shoulder, peering through the rain beating against the rear window so that he could reverse out of the parking slot. 'Still, if you're that disappointed, there's an obvious solution. I'm quite happy to leave you here. There's still time for you to get back on the plane!'

'Believe me, the idea has already crossed my mind,' Carey snapped, and Drew slowed down as he drove past the terminal entrance.

'Would you like me to drop you now?'

'What, and make your day?' she said, not bothering to disguise her sarcasm, and in spite of himself reluctant amusement tugged at Drew's mouth.

Carey didn't notice. She had a strong stubborn streak and Drew's hostility had only made her determined to stay, if only to prove that she couldn't be intimidated that easily. It might have been madness to let Camilla involve her in this ridiculous scheme, but now that she was here she was damned if she was going to let Drew Tarrant get the better of her! 'You needn't bother to stop,' she told Drew crisply. 'You may be desperate to get rid of me, but I've no intention of letting myself be bullied into going home before I've done what I came to do, so you'd better get used to me!'

The amusement vanished from Drew's expression and his eyes narrowed. 'Now *that* sounds more like the Camilla I was expecting!' Accelerating past the terminal, he drove out to the main road. It was so dark that he had switched his headlights on, although none of the other vehicles appeared to think that seeing or being seen was particularly worth bothering about. 'If you're determined to stay, I suppose there's not much I can do to stop you,' he said, waiting for a truck to shoot past, apparently careless of the fact that the rain had reduced visibility to a matter of feet. 'You won't get another chance to change your mind, though,' he warned Carey, who was clutching her seat nervously as he turned into the traffic. 'Our research is running behind schedule as it is, and I'm certainly not wasting any more time bringing you back to catch an earlier plane home if you decide you don't like it after all. As far as I'm concerned, you're a damned nuisance, and if you're expecting any special treatment you can forget it right now.'

'I'm not expecting anything from you,' said Carey haughtily.

'That's just as well, because you won't be getting anything,' said Drew. 'I don't want any whining about the conditions or how badly I'm treating you. If you come to Moonshadow Cay, you come on my terms. The cay isn't going to change for you, and neither am I.'

'Thanks for the welcome,' she said in an acid voice, and Drew glanced across at her with dislike.

'Just don't say I didn't warn you, that's all!'

CHAPTER TWO

THE crashing rain made it difficult to see much as they drove into Belize City. Carey had a confused impression of lush vegetation, weathered clapboard houses tilting on stilts and pot-holed streets, but it was doubtful whether she would have seen much more even if the sun had been blazing down. She was seething at the injustice of Drew's remarks and torn between the unpleasant realisation that she might have let herself in for more than she could handle and a stubborn determination to prove to Drew just how wrong he was.

Camilla would have handled him so much better, Carey couldn't help thinking. She had an extraordinary ability to coax even the most resistant men round to her way of thinking. The windscreen-wipers slapped frantically backwards and forwards in a futile attempt to sweep the rain away and Carey watched them, wondering how Camilla would have dealt with Drew Tarrant. She would have laughed at him, she decided, gaily refusing to let him provoke her. She *wouldn't* have lost her temper, as Carey had done. No, Camilla was far too clever for that. She would have relied on her beauty and her indubitable charm to cajole the hostile Dr Tarrant out of his hostility.

Carey cast Drew a sideways glance under her lashes, trying to imagine him a victim of Camilla's charm, but as her eyes fell on the inflexible line of his mouth and the uncompromising set of his jaw she wasn't so sure that Camilla would have had any more success than she had done. Drew Tarrant didn't look like the kind of man who would be susceptible to cajolery or charm. He didn't look as if he was susceptible to anything.

Suppressing a sigh, Carey turned her head away to gaze unseeingly out of the window. The only way she could imagine persuading Drew to regard her with a little less suspicion was to admit that she wasn't Camilla at all, but Camilla had made her promise faithfully that she wouldn't do anything of the kind. 'If anyone even *begins* to suspect you're not me, it's bound to get back to the office somehow, and that'll be the end of my career,' she had said, appalled at Carey's suggestion that there was no reason why the scientists shouldn't know who she really was. 'Promise you won't tell *anyone*, Carey!'

So Carey had promised, which meant that she was stuck with a hostile Drew Tarrant for the next two weeks. She wasn't looking forward to it. She just hoped his research assistant was a little more friendly!

They were bumping over an antiquated swing bridge in the middle of the city. 'Haulover Creek,' said Drew, turning down a side-road and bumping down a muddy track to a ramshackle-looking pier where a solitary open boat was tied up. A young Creole dressed only in shorts was cheerfully bailing out the rainwater, apparently unconcerned by the futile nature of his task.

'What are we doing here?' said Carey as Drew switched off the engine. She looked doubtfully at the creek. It looked dark, dirty and uninviting in the rain.

'That's my boat,' he replied, winding down the window and shouting something in Creole to the young man in the boat. Even through the rain, Carey could see his teeth flash in a wide smile as he clambered out of the boat and jogged along the jetty towards them.

'Boat?' echoed Carey, none the wiser, and Drew cast her an ironic look.

'How did you think we were going to get to Moonshadow Cay? Fly?'

'I hadn't thought about it,' she said honestly.

'Well, you can think about it now,' said Drew, reaching into the back seat for a voluminous waterproof cape. 'Francis and I are going to load the boat, and you're going to help us.'

'But it's raining!'

'I know it's raining,' he said irritably. 'But I'm not prepared to hang around until it clears up. It could be like this until tomorrow and I've wasted enough time picking you up as it is!' He got out and went round to the back of the car which was loaded up with crates of vegetables and jerricans and boxes of assorted supplies. Francis hoisted a crate in his arms and set off down to the boat while Carey gazed, appalled, at the amount of stuff.

'I'll be soaked by the time we've loaded up all this!' she protested.

'Does it matter?' said Drew with an unsympathetic look. 'You're wet already, aren't you? And Francis isn't complaining!'

'If it doesn't matter, how come *you've* provided yourself with a waterproof?' she demanded resentfully.

'I've come prepared ... and if you think I'm going to be a gentleman and offer it to you you've got another think coming!'

'Don't worry,' she snapped, grabbing the first box that came to hand. 'The thought that you would do anything remotely chivalrous hadn't even entered my mind!' The box was far too heavy for her, and she almost dropped it as she pulled it off the back of the car, but with Drew's sardonic eyes on her she refused to admit defeat, struggling instead down the muddy slope and staggering along the jetty, bent over with the weight of it. Still, she was relieved when Francis leapt nimbly up from the boat and took the box from her, and marched back up to the car with her head held high. Drew needn't think he could put her off that easily!

'What is all this stuff, anyway?' she asked, turning up the collar of Camilla's linen jacket in a vain attempt to keep out the rain.

'Supplies,' said Drew briefly. 'There's nothing on the island, so we have to bring everything in by boat. As I had to come in anyway to pick you up, it seemed a good chance to stock up.'

Carey opened her eyes at him. 'Surely you don't mean there was some advantage to my arrival today?'

'No, I don't mean that,' he said with an unpleasant look. 'If you hadn't come, I could have stayed on the cay and got on with some work. There's enough food to last a few days yet, but I don't intend coming in again until I can put you on the plane in two weeks' time.'

Sighing, Carey pulled another box towards her. The mud was slithery beneath her shoes and the jetty showed an alarming propensity to creak and list whenever she stepped on it, but she gritted her teeth and toiled up and down behind Drew while Francis stacked everything neatly in the boat and lashed a tarpaulin over it all.

Carey stood on the jetty and watched him tie the last few knots while she tried to recover her breath. It was all right if you were a tin of beans, she reflected as the rain dripped down her neck and ran in rivulets down her face. Right now, the idea of a dry box beneath the tarpaulin seemed the height of luxury, and she thought vengefully of Camilla, whose fault all this was, tucked up in her own clean, warm, dry little cottage.

'Right.' Drew checked that the tarpaulin was secure and tossed the car keys to Francis who caught them deftly. 'Francis will look after the car. Make sure you haven't left anything behind.'

'My camera!' Carey scrambled back up the slope and rescued her handbag and camera-bag that were sitting forlornly on the floor. They looked as wet and miserable and lost as she felt.

Francis swung himself into the driving seat and beamed at her. 'Have a good trip,' he said without the slightest trace of irony, and reversed the car back up the muddy track to the road.

Carey watched him out of sight before trailing back down to the jetty. Drew was rummaging in one of the lockers. 'Get in,' he said without looking up.

'Just a minute,' said Carey, keeping hold of her temper with difficulty, and he straightened impatiently.

'What is it?'

'How far is it to this Moonshadow Cay?'

He shrugged. 'A couple of hours. Maybe more in this weather.'

'Two hours in *that*?' Carey stared at him, aghast. The cays had looked so close to the coast on the map that she had imagined a trip of half an hour or so, not two hours at sea in an open boat!

'It'll get us there,' said Drew with one of his disconcerting gleams of amusement. 'It may not be up to your luxurious standards, but it's certainly the only way you are going to get there. Of course, you can always stay here if you'd prefer.'

Carey glared at him. 'I've no doubt that's what you would prefer! As it is, it doesn't look as if I've got much choice, does it?'

'No,' he said bluntly. 'Now, are you getting in or not?'

'Not until I've had something to eat,' said Carey, setting her jaw stubbornly.

Drew gave an exasperated sigh. 'I don't advise it.'

'I don't care whether you advise it or not,' she snapped. 'I haven't had anything to eat since I left Miami this morning, and I'm starving. And you needn't think you can abandon me here,' she swept on as Drew opened his mouth to protest. 'Not if you want Weatherill Willis to continue sponsoring your project, that is!'

Drew's mouth tightened. 'I wondered how long it would be before you brought up that particular piece of blackmail!' Slamming the locker shut, he swung himself up on to the jetty. 'Very well, have it your own way. I'm sure you're used to that! Just don't blame me if you regret it later.'

'Don't you think you're being a little unreasonable?' Carey demanded, trotting to keep up with him as he strode up to the road. There was nobody else out in the rain and she kept tripping over broken bits of pavement, which did nothing to improve her temper.

'Unreasonable?' Drew stopped so suddenly that she cannoned into him as he swung round on her savagely. 'Is it unreasonable to object to having an unscrupulous woman with a reputation for trouble-making thrust on my project for two weeks? Did *you* ever stop and think that it might not be convenient for you to come now? Of course you didn't! You just sent off your instructions—pick me up here, take me there—as if I had nothing better to do with my time than run around acting as a taxi service to a spoilt, bossy little madam who's sniffed out the scent of money and doesn't care about anything else!'

Carey's face was white with anger. 'Now, listen——'

'No, *you* listen!' he interrupted her, his eyes very clear and cold. 'Weatherill Willis offered a generous sponsorship deal and no scientific project is going to turn down extra money, but I'm funding most of this project myself. Anything they provide is a bonus, and I'd rather keep it if I can, but I'm certainly not dependent on it. I wouldn't have the slightest hesitation in telling Weatherill Willis where to put its money if you push your luck too far. You might remember that next time you try throwing your weight around, Miss Cavendish!'

'I was only asking for something to eat,' snapped Carey. Her eyes were huge and stormy, her wet hair plastered to her head. 'Is that so difficult?'

Drew had been glaring at her, but now he turned abruptly away with an exclamation of impatience. 'It's not *difficult*, it's just inconvenient and very unwise, but if you're so determined to get your own way you'd better hurry up. I'm not hanging around all day.' Striding up the street, he turned without warning into a dark, unmarked doorway which led straight up a flight of rickety wooden stairs.

Carey stared after him in impotent fury. She would have liked nothing better than to stalk away in the opposite direction, but she *was* hungry and, like it or not, she was utterly dependent on Drew Tarrant if she was to get to Moonshadow Cay and keep her promise to Camilla.

So she followed him up the stairs, trying to ignore the sinister darkness and not at all sure she wanted to know what was waiting for her at the top. Drew had disappeared through a door, and she hesitated before pushing it open. She found herself in a large, bare room, set with tables. To her surprise and slightly shamefaced relief, the room was full of people. It seemed this was a restaurant after all, evidently not one that relied on advertisements to pull in the customers.

Her gaze moved curiously around the room. At one end, a window was open to the rain. The paint was peeling off the shutters, one of which had come off its hinge and hung at a drunken angle, squeaking protestingly at the slightest breeze. Two naked light bulbs swung slightly in the draught of a slowly creaking ceiling fan. They threw an eerily shifting light over the dark room that merely added to the atmosphere of eccentric, dilapidated charm.

The air was hot and heavy, and Camilla's drenched suit felt clammy against Carey's skin. She could hear the rain drumming on the tin roof overhead. It seemed deafening at first, and it was only when her ears adjusted that she became aware that the entire room had fallen silent and was watching her standing wide-eyed in the doorway. Carey flushed, realising what a spectacle she must present with the rain still dripping from her suit, her hair hanging in rat's-tails about her face and her legs splattered with mud.

Biting her lip, she looked instinctively for Drew. He was standing at the far side of the room, and their eyes met across the tables with such a jolt that Carey almost took a step backwards. In the dim light, he looked oddly well-defined, clear and solid and somehow reassuring. His eyes were very light in his dark face. Carey read the mockery there and her chin came up instantly.

Conversation broke out as she walked across to Drew, head held high as if she were dressed in the latest style.

She thought she saw a flash of admiration in his eyes, but, if so, it was quickly shuttered.

'I've ordered you chicken and beans,' he said. 'It's a speciality, and you'll have enough fish on the cay.'

Carey's lips tightened. She would have preferred to order for herself, but there was no point in making a scene about it, so she sat down and peeled off her sodden jacket with relief, swivelling round to hang it off the back of her chair. She was anxious to check her camera. The bag was supposed to be waterproof, but it had never been exposed to anything like this rain before. Her face was intent as she examined her precious lenses, but fortunately they all seemed dry—certainly a lot drier than she was! Carey zipped the bag closed once more and set it down on the floor, wondering if she would ever feel dry again.

Straightening, she found Drew watching her and the breath stuck in her throat. He really did have extraordinary eyes, the cool, clear green even more striking between dark, almost sooty lashes. They held a peculiar expression. Carey thought she could read in them admiration as well as contempt, as much puzzlement as mockery, as if he was taken aback of his own ability to decide.

Then his gaze dropped and one eyebrow quirked. Instinctively following his look, Carey realised to her horror that the skimpy white silk top that had been so discreetly elegant when she'd put it on below the jacket that morning was now clinging to her body in a manner which revealed only too clearly that she wore no bra. Worse, it was so wet that it was practically see-through; she might as well have been sitting there naked!

The colour surged up Carey's cheeks as her appalled eyes met Drew's amused look and she compressed her lips furiously, dragging the jacket off the chair-back and pulling it back on with shaking hands. It was uncomfortably heavy, but anything was better than sitting there with Drew's unsettling eyes on her body. Her breasts seemed to be burning still where his eyes had rested and deep inside she could feel a flame of awareness flicker into alarming life.

'Very wise,' he commented ironically.

Carey eyed him with resentment. He had no right to be rude and unpleasant and then make her feel hot and flustered just by sitting there and *looking* like that. It wasn't as if there was anything special about him. He wasn't nearly as handsome as Giles, for instance, Carey reassured herself, although when she tried to remember exactly what Giles looked like his features seemed blurred.

There was nothing blurred about Drew Tarrant. His face was angular, his features peculiarly distinct, every line of his body decisive. He sat on the other side of the table, turning a glass of beer thoughtfully between his hands, the acute eyes veiled for once. Carey took the opportunity to study him, trying to work out what it was that made him so compelling. She had thought it was just the startling effect of his light eyes, but now she decided it was more than that. There was an air of steely self-containment about him, a sort of controlled assurance that set him apart from everyone else in the room.

Carey sensed a formidable intelligence and a reassuring competence, as if here was a man capable of making a success of whatever he put his mind to, but she couldn't help wondering what had put that watchful look in his eyes. She wondered, too, why a man successful enough to have had his own television series came to be sitting in this strange, dilapidated restaurant in his faded shirt. She wished now that she had seen his programmes. They must have shown a very different Drew Tarrant.

Absorbed in her thoughts, Carey was taken unawares when Drew lifted his head without warning and she found herself staring into eyes that were as green and cold as ice. The puzzled look they had held earlier had dissolved completely, as if he had been thinking about her while she had been watching him, and had made up his mind to dislike her after all. Carey felt as if a bucket of freezing water had been thrown in her face; the shock of it caught the breath in her throat and jolted her heart out of its steady rhythm so that her eyes widened even as his narrowed suspiciously.

'What's the matter?'

'Nothing,' she croaked, and cleared her throat hastily. 'That is, I was just wondering if it was true that you'd had your own television series.'

'There was a series, yes, but I wouldn't call it my own. It makes me sound like a chat-show host. It takes many different talents to make a natural-history programme. I wrote and narrated the programmes, but they wouldn't have been anything without the skill and patience of the rest of the team, particularly the camermen.'

'I heard it was a great success,' said Carey.

Drew shrugged and picked up his glass once more. 'I don't think any of us realised quite how successful a series it would be. My original intention was simply to increase awareness of the richness and complexity of marine life. The more people know and are interested in an area, the more willing sponsors are to support us. Weatherill Willis's sponsorship was a result of that programme, although sales of the books and videos of the series have put me in a position where I'm not reliant on sponsors any more.'

'I gathered that,' said Carey a little sourly, remembering how he had shouted at her in the street. 'Why do you bother with the hassles of sponsors at all if you don't need them?'

'Because the more money we have, the better our research will be. I might not be dependent on Weatherill Willis now, but I might well need sponsorship for other projects in the future, and it would be foolhardy not to take advantage of their offer, even if it does mean extra hassles. I'm a scientist, not a television personality, and I believe that what we're doing is vitally important. That means I'm prepared to do whatever's necessary to make sure we can continue our research as long as possible.'

'Even to the extent of putting up with me?'

'Up to a point,' said Drew with a cool look, and then broke off to smile up at the owner of the restaurant, a huge man with a broken boxer's nose. He was setting a plate piled high with refried beans and crispy chicken in front of Carey, who didn't even notice.

She was staring at Drew. She hadn't seen him smile before, and she was quite unprepared for the effect it would have. Just looking into his eyes had been shock enough, but it was nothing compared to how she felt now. The coolness that had seemed so much part of him had vanished with his smile. In its place was an animation and an unexpected humour that illuminated his features and made him look both younger and disconcertingly attractive. Suddenly Camilla's friend's opinion of him didn't seem so strange after all.

Carey felt very odd, as if everything about him had abruptly shifted focus. Unaware of her reaction, Drew was bantering with the owner. They obviously knew each other well, Carey thought, conscious of an absurd twinge of envy. Jerking her eyes away, she picked up her knife and fork and tried to concentrate on her food, but her gaze kept sliding back to Drew as if she had never seen him before. For the first time she noticed the laughter-lines starring his eyes and the way his smile deepened the creases in his cheeks. She noticed the warmth in his eyes and the curve of his long, firm mouth, and a strange feeling uncurled in the pit of her stomach.

Carey looked down at her chicken and realised that she wasn't hungry after all. The owner's attention was claimed at a nearby table and Drew turned back to her, the warmth fading from his face. Carey's heart sank to see the hardness return to his expression. He was as cool and implacable as before, and she wondered wildly if she had imagined the disquietingly attractive man he had been only seconds ago.

'Aren't you having anything to eat?' she asked awkwardly.

Drew shook his head. 'I'd rather wait until we get to the cay.'

Carey wished she had decided to do the same, but, having made such a fuss about eating, she could hardly change her mind now. She took a mouthful of chicken and chewed valiantly, very conscious of Drew watching her with those unsettling eyes of his.

'What brought you to Belize?' she asked at last, desperate to break the silence.

'The reef,' said Drew. 'I've been researching the ecology of coral reefs for several years now and the Belizean reef is one of the longest and most interesting. It's also one of the least developed, which makes it an ideal place for a comparative project.'

'What exactly are you doing?' Carey persevered.

'You wouldn't understand,' he said dismissively, and her eyes snapped.

'Try me.'

He glanced at her, surprised at her crisp tone. 'All right, if you insist.' He hesitated, and Carey could see him mentally trying to translate his research into layman's language. 'We're doing what we call a biodiversity survey of one particular area of the reef. That means recording as much data as possible about the different species that live on the reef and trying to understand how they interact, how they're affected by factors like pollution, hurricanes, changes in currents and so on.'

Drew had momentarily forgotten his dislike and leant forward, his face alight with enthusiasm. 'Coral reefs are often compared to rainforests in terms of age and complexity. It takes between five and ten thousand years for a reef to establish itself, and during that time it evolves into an incredibly intricate system supporting thousands of different species, few of which we know very much about. My particular interest is in the function of bright colours in tropical fish—are they used as a warning, or a confusing signal to predators, or are they simply to attract a mate? Are there different-coloured varieties of one species, or is it the same fish changing colours according to mood? Do——?'

He broke off suddenly, as if realising that he had allowed his fascination for the subject to carry him away. 'That kind of thing,' he finished abruptly.

'I see.' Carey had been enjoying the animation in his face and was stung by the obvious way he had remembered how much he disliked her. 'Tell me,' she asked sweetly, 'what exactly did you think I wouldn't understand in all that? Or did you think that I wouldn't be able to cope with words of more than one syllable?'

Drew's brows snapped together and he glared at her. 'Perhaps it would have been more accurate to have said that I didn't think you'd be interested.'

'I wouldn't have asked if I hadn't been interested,' said Carey, ploughing on through the pile of beans, but Drew only gave a snort of disbelief.

'If you were *interested* in our work, you wouldn't even consider the idea of a resort on the cay,' he said scathingly. 'The only thing people like you are interested in is money.'

Carey put down her fork with an exasperated click and pushed her plate aside. 'You seem to forget that companies like Weatherill Willis—*people like me*, after all—provide valuable sponsorship for hundreds of scientific projects. You may not need their money, but other scientists do. Surely the fact that they—*we*—sponsor you at all shows an interest in the environment and research?'

'Oh, I dare say you all know the right words to mouth about conservation now that it's become a fashionable issue, but you're not seriously asking me to believe that a company like Weatherill Willis would sponsor us if it wasn't getting something out of it itself? It probably recoups it all in tax concessions.'

Carey's eyes were grey and direct. 'You're very cynical.'

'Perhaps,' he said indifferently. 'I prefer to think of it as being realistic.'

'"Realistic" isn't the word I'd use to describe someone who takes money from people he makes no secret of despising!'

She had got through to him at last. Anger flared in Drew's eyes and his mouth set in a fierce line. 'And why are *you* here?' he retorted. 'You're not here because of any concern about the environment or any deep-seated interest in marine life. No, you're here because you think you can make money out of the cay, so don't try and take a moral line with me.' He looked her up and down contemptuously. 'I've met girls like you before, girls who look sweet but have calculators for hearts, and I've found it pays to be realistic—or cynical, if you prefer—about them right from the start.'

'I'm not like that at all!' said Carey indignantly. 'You can't just make up your mind about people based on some stupid prejudice.'

'I make up my mind based on experience,' said Drew with a cool look. 'And nothing about you, Camilla Cavendish, is likely to convince me to change it.'

Outside the rain was still falling steadily, although it seemed to Carey that it wasn't quite as overpowering. Either it had slackened off or she was getting used to it, she thought as she squelched behind Drew back to the boat.

She waited on the jetty while Drew bailed out the rainwater that had gathered at the bottom of the boat, wondering why he was bothering. It was only going to fill up again. Her heart sank at the thought of the two uncomfortable hours that lay ahead and she thought again of Camilla who had gaily assured her that she would have an idyllic fortnight in the Caribbean sun. Carey stood on the ramshackle pier and reflected that she had rarely been in a less idyllic situation.

'OK.' Drew straightened at last and tossed the bailer down. 'You can get in now.'

Carey hesitated. The weight of the supplies had left the boat lying low in the water and it was an awkward drop down, quite apart from the way the tide was rocking the boat alarmingly against the jetty.

'What is it now?' Drew demanded irritably, looking up from the engine.

'Are you sure this is safe?' Carey cast a doubtful look at the laden boat.

'Of course it's safe,' he said in exasperation. With a sigh, he stepped over a crate and held up an impatient hand to her. 'I'm not wasting any more time here. Hurry up and get in or I'll leave you behind, sponsorship or no sponsorship!'

Swallowing, Carey took his hand and felt his fingers close around hers. They were cool and firm and very strong and she looked down at them, surprised at how reassured she felt by his touch.

'Come *on*!' snapped Drew, who was patently not prepared to stand around holding her hand while she thought about how it felt. 'Jump!'

Carey jumped. She would have stumbled and fallen on to the boxes if he hadn't held her in an iron grip and set her back on her feet.

'Look what you're doing!' he said with some asperity. 'You'll have all my stores overboard if you blunder around like that!'

'And I suppose it doesn't matter if I fall overboard?' she snapped, thoroughly unnerved by the realisation that she didn't want to let go of his hand.

'At least I could have fished you out again, which is more than I could have done with all those cans of baked beans.' The seats ran round the sides above the lockers, but there were so many boxes and crates spread evenly over the bottom of the boat that Carey had been left only a small space to squeeze in towards the stern. 'Sit down there,' Drew ordered, pointing, and she took her place reluctantly while he made his way forward and cast off at the bow.

He had plenty of room, Carey noted crossly as he returned to the stern to start the outboard. It roared into life and then settled down to idle muttering as Drew leant over her to cast off at the rear. He was utterly at home in the boat, moving with a balanced ease in the cramped space, and when he sat down at last to take the throttle he looked perfectly comfortable.

Carey huddled against a crate and eyed him resentfully. It was all right for him, she thought, blinking the rain out of her eyes and sniffing. He had a cape to keep off the rain.

'Have you got another cape I can borrow?' she asked as Drew eased open the throttle and pointed the boat out towards the sea.

He glanced at her impatiently, then stood up to flip open the locker beneath him. Keeping his hand on the throttle, he scrabbled around until he produced a couple of black rubbish bags. 'This is the best I can do,' he said, tossing them across to her.

Carey caught them clumsily, staring down at the plastic in her hands as he sat back down. 'What am I supposed to do with these?'

'Use your initiative,' said Drew unhelpfully. 'I haven't got anything else to give you.'

Camilla wouldn't have given up until he had given her his cape, Carey reflected with an inward sigh. Unfortunately, she didn't have Camilla's persistence, nor her thick skin. Drew wouldn't give it to her anyway, and Carey was damned if she would give him the satisfaction of pleading.

She managed at last to tear a hole in the bottom of one the bags, and poked two more holes through for her arms. When she had wriggled into it, she ripped the other one into two. One piece she spread over her lap, the other she fashioned into a sort of hood. It wasn't very effective, but she supposed it was better than nothing.

'I don't know why you don't have a boat with a bit of shelter,' she grumbled, tucking the ends of the plastic around her knees.

'It's not worth it,' he said with a malicious look at the rain running down her face. 'We only come out for the dry season; we spend the rest of the year in the laboratories collating our research.'

Carey wiped her cheeks with the back of her hand. 'Why are you out here now, then?'

'This is the dry season.'

'You could have fooled me,' said Carey with a sigh, watching the rain stream off her hood on to her lap and thence neatly down on to her feet.

Her expression was such an accurate mirror of her thoughts that Drew couldn't help grinning. 'Welcome to the Caribbean!'

Carey threw him a haughty look, fully intending to show him how much she resented his obvious enjoyment of her misery, but the glinting amusement in his eyes was irresistible. She must look ridiculous, she realised ruefully, wedged like a drowning rat between the crates in ragged plastic, ankle-deep in water. Was it only a couple of hours ago that she had stepped off the plane in her sophisticated suit? No wonder he found the transformation so amusing! Their eyes met across the crate and somehow Carey's defiant look turned into a reluctant answering grin.

Suddenly the rain didn't seem to matter. Drew was smiling at her, and as Carey smiled back at him through the rain something quite unexpected seemed to leap into life between them, like a needle swinging inexorably round to point north when you were convinced you were heading south. It wasn't liking, thought Carey, peculiarly shaken, but something more like recognition. She knew that Drew felt it too; she could see the flicker in his eyes as if he too was taken aback by the odd, disturbing sense of affinity.

For a long moment it held them immobile while their smiles faded uncertainly, until, with an identical effort, they jerked their eyes apart. Carey stared down at her hands, wondering how it was possible to feel such a magnetic pull towards someone she disliked as much as she disliked Drew Tarrant. She could just see him out of the corner of her eye. She didn't want to look at him, but something about him kept tugging at her gaze, and suddenly it seemed terribly important not to give in and look after all. Carey was convinced that if she did she would lose control of herself altogether. She had a bizarre image of herself being drawn helplessly against his hard body, like iron to magnet, and the fact that she could imagine it quite so clearly she found most frightening of all.

This was Drew Tarrant, she reminded herself frantically. He had been arrogant, unpleasant, unwelcoming, downright rude, and she hated him. She should be remembering that, instead of letting her imagination run wild just because of a smile. Drew might find her predicament amusing, but he had made no secret of the fact that he disliked her quite as much as she disliked him. Carey told herself with a strangely sinking heart that she would be a fool to forget it.

CHAPTER THREE

THE little boat emerged from the shelter of the creek into the open sea and began juddering over the choppy waves. Every now and then they would hit a bigger one and the spray would surge over the side to land with uncanny accuracy on the back of Carey's neck.

Carey thought she had been wet before, but it was nothing compared to this comprehensive drenching every few minutes. There was no point in complaining to Drew, though, so she gritted her teeth and closed her eyes at each deluge. Her plastic 'hood' was worse than useless and after a while she gave up the effort of trying to keep it over her head.

'What's the matter?' enquired Drew maliciously. 'Waterproofs not up to standard?'

Carey shot him a look of acute dislike, marvelling that she could have wasted so much as a moment worrying about being drawn to him. 'What on earth gives you that idea?' she asked sarcastically. 'Surely you don't think I'd be rude enough to complain about these wonderful dustbin bags you so thoughtfully provided for me?'

'I'm glad you like them,' said Drew suavely, an appreciative gleam in his eyes.

'Oh, I'll treasure them,' she assured him through clenched teeth. 'They'll always remind me of my warm welcome to Belize!'

'If you're trying to needle me into giving you my cape, I'm afraid you're wasting your breath,' he retorted in a

43

deceptively pleasant voice, and Carey eyed him with ill-concealed hostility.

'I don't want your rotten cape!' she said, folding her arms crossly. 'I'm so wet now that I might as well give in and swim the rest of the way. It couldn't make me any wetter!'

But as the long minutes passed and the waves continued to break over her, she found herself getting colder and colder. The air had been hot and humid in the town, but the sea breeze chilled the wet clothes against her skin and she huddled down in her seat, trying to shelter from the wind behind the meagre protection of the crates.

They seemed to be heading straight out into the sea, and the further they got, the choppier the waves became. Drew sat at the tiller, still and self-contained beneath his cape, his eyes narrowed slightly against the rain but otherwise indifferent to the miserable conditions. To Carey he looked like a rock, the only solid thing in this wet, watery seascape. Occasionally tiny islands would emerge out of the rain and Carey's hopes would rise, only to be dashed as the boat puttered past and on into the empty water.

It wasn't long before Carey began to realise why Drew had advised her against eating, either. She had never suffered from seasickness before, but the combination of the boat's jolting progress over the waves, tiredness and the refried beans settling in a stomach already disorientated by the time changes during the flight from England was making her feel distinctly queasy.

Carey wrapped her arms around herself in a vain attempt to stop her stomach heaving and glared at Drew, convinced that he had arranged things deliberately. She wouldn't put it past him to have laid on the rain specially and to have been personally responsible for whipping up the waves, just to make her miserable. And he had ordered the beans...

At the thought of the beans, Carey's stomach lurched and she bit down hard on her lip.

'Feeling rough?' Drew shouted over the noise of the outboard, and her chin came up. She wouldn't give him the satisfaction of knowing just how revolting she felt.

'No,' she lied with dignity, and promptly lunged to the other side of the boat where she was thoroughly, humiliatingly, sick into the sea.

When it was all over she crouched back in her seat, shivering, and took the bottle of water Drew handed her wordlessly to rinse out her mouth.

'You'll feel better for that,' he said with what Carey considered an utterly callous lack of sympathy.

'Oh, yes, I feel marvellous!' she snapped, screwing the top back on the bottle. 'Never better! I'm cold and wet and sick in an open boat in the pouring rain with the most heartless, despicable, *hateful* man I've ever had the misfortune to meet, and if you *dare* to say that I chose to come with you I...I'll push you overboard!'

Unexpectedly, amusement stirred in Drew's green eyes and the cleft at the corner of his mouth deepened as if he was trying not to grin. Carey looked at it with loathing, too cold and miserable to feel anything other than fury that he dared to find her funny.

'All right, I won't say it, then,' he said equably. 'But I *did* warn you not to have anything to eat, didn't I?'

'If I'd known it was going to be like this, I wouldn't have eaten anything,' said Carey sulkily. Sighing, she rubbed her hands up and down her arms in a vain effort to get warm. 'How much longer till we get there?'

'About an hour.'

'Another hour?' she cried, appalled. 'I thought you said it would only take a couple of hours altogether? We must have been out here for at least three—or are we going round in circles?'

Drew sent her another disconcertingly amused look. 'I sincerely hope not! By my reckoning, we're about halfway.'

'You mean we've only been going an hour?' To her horror, Carey found that tears were very close. She felt as if she had been stuck in the boat forever and the prospect of another hour like the last one was too much to contemplate.

'That's right.' Drew looked at her sharply, hearing the tell-tale waver in her voice, but she refused to cry. That would just make his day! Instead she clenched her jaw and stared defiantly back at him with eyes that were huge and grey in her pinched white face.

He gave an exasperated sigh and untied his cape where it fastened at the neck. 'Here, you'd better come under this and get warm,' he said in a resigned tone, holding the cape open invitingly.

'No, thank you,' said Carey haughtily. Did he really think she had been just waiting to snuggle up to him?

'Don't be ridiculous, woman!' Drew snapped. 'Pride won't keep you very warm for the next hour.'

'It didn't seem to bother you before!'

'Well, it's bothering me now,' he said in exasperation, reaching across to seize Carey's wrist. Before she had time to protest, he had pulled her roughly across and down on to the seat beside him and flung the cape over her shoulders so that they were both sheltered beneath its voluminous folds.

Seriously ruffled by finding herself so impatiently hauled against him, Carey scowled and held herself stiffly away from his body, but it was almost impossible in the confines of the cape, and after a minute or so Drew gave another exasperated sigh.

'For heaven's sake!' he growled, and put his arm around her shoulders to draw her firmly against his side and wrap them tightly together.

'I'll make you all wet,' said Carey, a little breathless.

'That ought to make you feel better, then,' said Drew.

But it didn't. Only a few moments ago, Carey had been slumped wretchedly between her crates, convinced that anything would be an improvement on her circumstances. Now she half wished she was back there. The cape was heavier than she'd expected and effectively kept out the wind and the spray while Drew's body warmed her, but his nearness was infinitely disturbing. Before, the cold and the wet had preoccupied her; now she had nothing to think about but how warm and hard and solid his body was. The arm around her shoulders had a steely strength that comforted her even as his closeness threw her senses into jittery disarray.

Drew himself might as well have had his arm round a sack of potatoes for all the notice he took of her. His other hand rested on the throttle, his eyes squinted through the rain, and he seemed absorbed in thought. Insensibly reassured by his patent lack of interest, Carey allowed herself to relax against him. After a while she felt peculiarly comfortable tucked into his side...almost *right*.

The thought made her frown and she glanced up at Drew, confused by the way he managed to make her feel secure and uneasy at the same time. He was staring ahead through the rain, the straight brows drawn slightly together over his nose. From this angle she could see only the decisive line of his jaw and one corner of that firm, strangely exciting mouth. He had pulled down the hood of the cape so that she could shelter beneath it as well and she watched a raindrop trickle from the hair at his temple over his cheek and down past his jaw to his throat.

Carey tingled with the sudden need to reach up and stop its progress, to feel his skin beneath her fingers and keep out the rain by burrowing her face into the tempting hollow between his jaw and throat.

Appalled at the train of her own thoughts, she dragged her gaze away, but she was so close to him that it was impossible to stop thinking about him. She wished she knew what made him so suspicious of her, or rather of Camilla, since that was who he believed her to be. Carey thought she could understand why Drew distrusted the whole idea of developing the island—she was even sympathetic to his point of view—but there was something more personal behind his bitter distrust of Camilla, almost as if he were a discarded lover. But of course he couldn't be. Camilla would have recognised his name, for a start, and if he had ever met her cousin he would have known at once that she was an imposter, Carey reassured herself, choosing not to analyse why she was quite so anxious to be convinced that Drew could never have been in love with Camilla.

He wasn't Camilla's type, anyway... but was she his? Carey stole another glance up at his unyielding profile. What kind of woman would he find attractive? Warm and vivacious, or cool and elegant? Whichever, he was the kind of man who would have whatever he wanted, Carey decided, then wondered if she was right after all as she remembered how cynical he had sounded in the restaurant. Had he been hurt in the past? Was he still hurt, or had some girl succeeded in convincing him that

all women were not the same? Was there someone—a
wife?—waiting patiently for him to come home?
Something twisted inside her at the thought, and, realising suddenly how comfortably she was nestled against
him, Carey flushed and straightened.

'That's Moonshadow Cay up ahead.' Drew's words
were a welcome distraction, and she peered across the
water at a bedraggled little island, shrouded in rain.

Drew withdrew his arm to concentrate on taking the
boat carefully through a gap in the reef, and Carey
slipped back to her place between the crates so that he
was free to manoeuvre. A ramshackle wooden jetty jutted
out into the lagoon from the shore. Drew eased the boat
alongside, and stepped out to tie it up securely. Turning
back to the boat, he hesitated, looking down at Carey
who was still sitting numb and white-faced on the seat,
hardly able to believe that they had arrived at last, and
reached down a hand to help her out.

'You go on up,' he said brusquely, jerking his head
towards a collection of thatched huts that stood in a
clearing beneath the coconut palms.

'What about all the stuff?' Carey asked, dropping his
hand as soon as she could and trying to rub some feeling
into her backside, which was feeling the effect of two
and a half hours on an uncomfortable wooden seat.

'I'll bring it up. You go and get dry.'

Carey shot him a suspicious look. It wasn't like Drew
to be so considerate. 'I've lasted this long,' she said after
a tiny pause. 'I dare say I'll last a few minutes longer
without dissolving, and it'll be much quicker if I give
you a hand.'

There was a flash of surprise in Drew's eyes and for
a moment she thought he was going to object, but then

he nodded abruptly and jumped back into the boat to untie the tarpaulin.

Carey plodded doggedly backwards and forwards between the boat and the hut used for stores. The boxes felt even heavier than before, and she was so stiff and tired that she was convinced her legs were going to give way beneath her. Drew carried twice as much and managed to complete two trips in the time it took her to do one, but Carey simply gritted her teeth and persevered. When at last they were finished, she was rewarded by a look that was almost respect in Drew's eyes.

'You're tougher than you look, Camilla.'

'Carey,' she reminded him tiredly. 'I'd rather you called me Carey.'

Drew straightened from stacking the last box and looked at her. She was slumped helplessly against the door of the hut, grey eyes enormous and dull with exhaustion. He frowned. 'All right, *Carey*,' he said gruffly, taking her arm. 'Come on, we'd better get you dry.'

His strength seemed to flow through his grip on her as he led her across to the largest hut. Propped up on stilts, it had bamboo walls and a thatched roof. A flight of wooden steps led up to a narrow veranda and if Drew hadn't been holding her Carey didn't think she would have made it.

Inside, the hut was spartanly furnished with two tables, one of them piled high with notebooks, papers and a lap-top computer, a couple of wicker armchairs and a bench which obviously served as a kitchen, with two gas burners connected to a bottle. At the back, a beaded curtain led through into another room.

Drew hooked a stool out from beneath the table with his foot and pushed Carey gently down on to it. Lighting one of the burners, he set a battered kettle on to boil, but when he turned back Carey was sitting exactly where he had left her, water still dripping from her wet clothes to make a puddle around her on the floor.

Carey herself felt curiously detached. She knew she should try and dry herself, but the last burst of defiant energy unloading the boat had utterly exhausted her, and now that she had stopped she didn't seem to be able to move. A corner of her mind recognised that this numbness stemmed from tiredness. She seemed to have been on the move ever since she'd left Yorkshire. She had spent last night in Miami but she had been so disorientated by the long flight that she hadn't slept well, and she had had to be up early this morning to catch the connecting flight to Belize. Now all she could do was sit here and drip and wonder what Camilla would say when she saw her suit. It would never be the same again.

Drew muttered something under his breath and disappeared through the bead curtain, to emerge a few seconds later with a towel. Tossing it down on the table, he ordered Carey to take off her jacket.

'No,' she roused herself to say, remembering how revealing the top had been before, but Drew brushed her protests aside.

'Don't be stupid, woman. I've got too much on my mind to waste time leering at your body, and you'll never get dry with this thing on.' He peeled it firmly from first one arm and then the other, and dropped it without ceremony on the floor, before taking the towel and rubbing her hair vigorously.

Carey succumbed at first, but as her circulation came back her muffled protests could be heard beneath the towel, and when Drew took pity on her at last and let her go the dullness had gone from her eyes. Instead they were bright and cross as she emerged from beneath the towel, mopping the last wetness from her face and rubbing her ear gingerly.

'Did you have to be quite so rough?'

Drew studied her impersonally. Her hair was hopelessly tousled about her face, but her skin was glowing again. 'I thought you needed a little shock treatment to get your blood moving again. It worked, didn't it?'

It *had* worked, but Carey didn't feel like admitting as much. She sniffed and turned her face ostentatiously away, but when she glanced back he was watching her with the same gleam of amusement that had had such a strange effect on her before. Sure enough, Carey found a reluctant smile tugging at her own mouth just as it had on the boat when she had wanted to hate him but could only share his amusement.

'Oh, all right,' she said, trying, and failing, to sound cross. 'It worked. I feel better.'

'Good.' Drew was leaning back against the bench, arms folded as he observed her, long legs crossed at the ankles. Their eyes met and the same sense of peculiar recognition dried the breath without warning in Carey's throat. It was very quiet. In the silence, she could hear the rain pattering on the roof, but it seemed to come from a long way away. It was as if the air between them was stretching and twanging with a new, unexpected tension, and Carey found that she was holding herself so tautly that when the kettle gave a shrill whistle she jumped.

Drew straightened unhurriedly and turned away to pour boiling water into two chipped enamel mugs. He handed one to Carey. 'Tea,' he said, so casually that Carey wondered if she had imagined it all. 'There's no milk, I'm afraid, but it will warm you up.'

Carey took the mug from him carefully, very conscious of her fingers brushing against his with a disquieting thrill of awareness. 'Thank you.' Shocked at how hoarse her voice sounded, she cleared her throat and got to her feet, unable to sit still any longer. Cupping her hands around the mug, she prowled nervously around the hut, the towel draped around her neck. The silence was making her uneasy.

Drew seemed quite comfortable with it. He had resumed his relaxed position against the bench and was watching her restless progress with those disconcertingly light eyes of his.

Conscious of his stare, but determined to ignore it, Carey parted the bead curtain and peered through into a small, windowless room which was only just large enough to accommodate two camp beds separated by an upturned crate. A sleeping-bag was spread over one of the beds, and a torch stood next to an alarm clock on the crate. This must be where Drew slept.

Carey was disturbed by how vividly she could imagine him lying there and she stepped back, dropping her hand abruptly from the curtain so that the beads clicked back together. She turned back to face Drew.

'Where shall I put my things?' Her suitcase and camera-bag, having been snugly tucked away under the tarpaulin, were barely damp and stood by the door with her handbag, which hadn't, squashed limply on top of them.

Drew looked surprised and jerked his head at the bead curtain, still whispering back into place. 'In there.'

'But...isn't that your room?'

'Yes.'

Carey set her mug very carefully down on the table. 'Do you mean I have to *sleep* with you?'

The sneer was back in Drew's eyes. 'What's the matter? You can't tell me that you of all people haven't slept with a man before?'

She flushed and set her teeth. 'I've certainly never slept with anyone as unpleasant as you!'

'There's a first time for everything,' said Drew, unperturbed.

'But what about the other huts?' said Carey, ruffled. 'Why can't I sleep in one of those?'

'Because it's not convenient,' he said curtly. 'The other huts are full of stores and samples and diving equipment, and I'm not having you blundering around in them.'

Carey pressed her lips together and picked up her mug once more. 'I don't understand,' she complained. 'I thought you had an assistant. Where does he sleep? In fact, where *is* he?' she asked, looking around her as if realising for the first time that no one else had appeared.

Drew's expression was shuttered. 'He's in England. He's taken some samples back to analyse in the labs.'

'Oh.' Realisation dawned slowly. 'So we're alone?'

He gave a grim smile. 'Quite alone.'

Alone with Drew Tarrant. The thought sent a shiver that was not quite fear, not quite excitement down Carey's spine. Her hands felt unsteady and she gripped them around the mug so that Drew shouldn't guess how they were shaking.

'I see.'

She stood by the table, biting her lip as she eyed him uncertainly. Her hair was drying in a tumbled cloud around her fine-boned face and her grey eyes were huge and wary. The white linen skirt still clung damply to her slender figure, while the towel slung round her shoulders decorously covered the skimpy and embarrassingly revealing sleeveless top.

'There's no need to look so nervous,' said Drew in a hard voice, reading her thoughts with tolerable accuracy. 'I expect I'll be able to keep my hands off you.'

His jeering tone was enough to replace the wariness in Carey's expression with a spark of anger, and she lifted her chin in a characteristic gesture. 'I'm not worried about *that*!'

'Why not?'

She glared at him. 'You haven't made any secret of the fact that you dislike me. I don't know what I've done to deserve such hostility, but at least it means I'm not afraid you're going to pounce on me!'

'It doesn't necessarily follow,' said Drew, straightening from his relaxed position lounging against the bench and putting down his mug. 'The fact that I distrust everything about you doesn't stop me noticing your undoubted charms.' His eyes travelled over her in an impersonal scrutiny that brought a flush to Carey's cheeks. 'I must admit that when I first saw you I thought rumour had exaggerated your seductive appeal. I was expecting someone a lot more obvious, but now that I look at you properly I can see that you're really rather beautiful in an understated sort of way.'

Carey's jaw dropped. Camilla had always been the beautiful one, Carey only ever a pale imitation of her, overshadowed by her cousin's flamboyant looks. Camilla was always telling her that she didn't make the best of herself, but it always seemed like so much effort that Carey was content to remain as she was. She would never be striking or exotic like Camilla, but she knew that she was attractive enough. She had never considered herself beautiful, though, and she certainly didn't feel it now, with her hair drying in a tangled mess and Camilla's skirt sticking uncomfortably to her skin.

She was so obviously astonished that Drew's brows drew together in a suspicious frown. 'Why the surprise?' he demanded, looking at her more closely. 'A girl like you usually takes compliments as her due.'

'I was merely surprised to get any compliment at all from *you*,' Carey retorted, recovering herself enough to realise that she couldn't afford to be too different from Camilla. Drew's picture of her might be exaggerated, but it held a kernel of truth, and it wouldn't do for him to get too suspicious. She finished her tea with a show of unconcern and put the mug down on the table. 'I'd like to wash,' she said, trying to sound dignified.

To her relief, Drew seemed to accept the change of subject, and the suspicious look in his eyes dissolved into a glint of humour. 'What? Aren't you wet enough?'

Carey couldn't resist a rueful smile back. 'Wet but not clean,' she said, grimacing down at herself. 'What I'd really like is a long, hot bath, but I don't suppose I'm going to get one?'

'You suppose right,' said Drew with an amused look at her resigned expression. 'We might be surrounded by sea, but fresh water is a problem on an island like this. There's a brackish well for emergencies, but most of the water has to be brought in by boat, so it's strictly rationed. You can have some to wash with, but please be careful with it.' Beckoning her over to the doorway, he pointed at a rough wicker hut set apart from the storerooms. 'That's our bathroom. You'll find soap and water in there, and there's a latrine round the back. Rather primitive, I'm afraid, but you'll just have to make the best of it. This isn't a hotel.'

'Really?' Carey opened her eyes at him with exaggerated innocence. 'The charming service had me fooled there for a minute!'

They were standing together in the doorway, and Drew looked down at her, exasperation warring with a reluctant respect and amusement in his eyes. Amusement won, and he gave in and grinned.

'I warn you, the restaurant facilities don't match up to the standard of accommodation!'

His smile seemed to burn behind Carey's eyelids as she washed, and brushed her teeth. It was a glorious relief to strip off her sodden clothes at last, but for some reason she was very conscious of her naked body, and she hurriedly pulled on a pair of loose cotton trousers and a demure short-sleeved blouse. She had no intention of revealing any more of herself to Drew's sharp eyes.

Dragging a comb ruthlessly through her tangled hair, Carey scowled. It wasn't fair of him to smile like that just when she had decided that he was thoroughly unpleasant! She felt edgy and unsettled whenever she thought about Drew. She wished she couldn't picture him quite so clearly. He might as well have been in the room with her. She tried to remember how horrible he had been to her, but kept remembering instead how strong his hand had been and the way the smile glimmered in his eyes. His abrupt changes of mood baffled her. One minute he looked at her as if he despised her, the next he seemed to if not actually *like* her, at least to be reluctantly revising his opinion of her. Carey just hoped he was as confused as she was!

The camp beds kept catching at the corner of her eye. They were awfully close. How was she going to lie there tonight, knowing that Drew was only inches away? They might as well be in the same bed!

Carey was no prude but the thought of sharing a room with Drew made her more nervous than she cared to admit, even to herself. It wasn't that she was afraid he would jump on her—he had made his lack of interest clear enough on *that* score! No, it was just that he was so...so hard to ignore. His body had been rock-solid and very strong when he had held her against him beneath the cape. Carey wished she couldn't remember it quite so clearly.

She wished she couldn't imagine how it would feel to be held against his skin.

She burned at the thought. She could feel her nerves quiver in anticipation...*anticipation*? What was she thinking of? Jerking her head up, Carey took an abrupt step back from the beds as if they had snapped at her. It was intolerable that she should be asked to sleep so close to a man who was, after all, a perfect stranger. She would rather sleep outside, and if it ever stopped raining that was what she would do!

Carey took a deep breath and smoothed her slickly combed hair behind her ears. The last thing she wanted was for Drew to guess how much the thought of sleeping beside him disturbed her. He would love *that*! No, she would be cool and polite and let him think she was utterly unconcerned by the prospect, and with any luck he would be the one feeling awkward.

Not that he ever would, Carey thought resentfully as she sat opposite him at the table. It was quite dark by then and he had lit a kerosene lamp which hissed and spluttered, throwing flickering shadows over their faces. Drew was too coolly self-possessed ever to feel awkward about anything. He had heated up a tin of stew with some rice. It wasn't very nice, but Carey was hungry enough to eat anything by then. Drew himself was unbothered by the taut silences, but Carey felt obliged to keep up a flow of polite and brittle conversation just to prove to him that she wasn't bothered either. Typically, she got little help from Drew who saw no need to keep up his side of the conversation and contented himself with terse replies. By the time the meal was over, Carey felt exhausted with the sheer effort of appearing relaxed, and she leapt up to carry the plates across to the bench while she thought of something else to say. The hut had evidently been put together in a very rough-and-ready fashion, for she could see the faint, pale gleam of sand between the floorboards.

'Why are all the huts built on stilts?' she asked, wondering if her voice always sounded that high and artificial.

'To keep out snakes mostly,' said Drew laconically, and Carey's voice rose even higher.

'*Snakes*?'

'You get boa constrictors on some of these islands,' he said in the same casual tone he might use to mention sheep on a farm or ducks on a pond.

Carey's eyes bulged. '*Boa constrictors*?' she echoed in a horrified squeak. 'You're not serious!'

'Of course I am,' said Drew, looking faintly surprised. 'They don't grow very big here, though, so you don't need to worry. They wouldn't take anything bigger than a small dog.'

They sounded big enough to Carey. Swallowing, she abandoned all ideas of sleeping out under the stars. Right now, wild horses wouldn't drag her down those steps and out of the hut. Sleeping with Drew might be a disturbing prospect, but it wasn't *that* disturbing!

Across the room, her appalled gaze met Drew's. Was he pulling her leg? He sat poker-faced at the table, but there was a distinct glint of derision in his eyes and Carey was suddenly sure that he could read her mind and knew exactly how nervous she was at the thought of sleeping

in the same room as him, in spite of her brave attempt
to appear carelessly unconcerned. It wasn't a comfortable
feeling and, not for the first time, she wished he didn't
have such an unnervingly perceptive look about him.

Tearing her eyes away from his, she fiddled with her
watch-strap, very conscious of him watching her in a
silence that grew ever tauter as the seconds passed. Carey
could hear the rain whispering on the thatch while she
searched her mind desperately for something else to say.
She knew that if she didn't she would just glance back
at Drew and she was horribly afraid that this time she
would not be able to look away.

'This is a very small hut for two people to spend much
time in together,' she said on a sort of gasp. 'Don't you
and your assistant ever get on each other's nerves?'

'We get on very well,' said Drew curtly. 'One of us is
often away doing comparative studies on another part
of the reef, and even if we are here together it rarely
rains like this, so we're not stuck inside.'

Carey determinedly resisted the impulse to look at him.
'Is he nice, your assistant?' she persevered. 'What's his
name?'

There was a tiny pause. 'Paul,' said Drew at last, very
distinctly. 'Paul Jarman.'

There was something significant in the way he spoke,
as if he expected her to react in some way. Carey risked
an uncertain glance at Drew, who was watching her with
an unmistakably contemptuous expression.

'Oh,' she said cautiously, not at all sure what else she
could say, and then flinched as Drew got abruptly to his
feet, scraping the stool back across the floorboards, to
stare at her. Baffled, she could only look nervously back
at him, wondering what she had said, or not said. There

was an explosive air about him, as if he was about to erupt with rage, but when he spoke it was with a menacing softness.

'You don't even remember, do you?'

CHAPTER FOUR

'REMEMBER?' Carey stared blankly at him. 'Remember what?'

Drew searched her face with hard, incredulous eyes. 'Paul...you really don't remember him, do you?'

'Er...no,' she said, moistening her lips nervously. Oh, God, this was something else Camilla hadn't warned her about! What was it she had said? 'Nobody in Belize is going to know who I am.' If she ever got out of this stupid mess, Carey thought vengefully, she would never believe anything Camilla said ever again. 'Should I?'

'I would have thought there might be some deeply buried shred of decency in you somewhere that would bother to remember the lives you've ruined!' sneered Drew. 'Still, I suppose it makes it easier for you to sleep at night!'

Carey drew herself up to her full height. If this was something to do with Camilla she had better find out what it was, although she suspected she wasn't going to like what she heard. 'Would you like to tell me what you're talking about?' she said icily.

'All right, since your memory seems to be so conveniently blank.' Drew propped himself against the table and folded his arms with an ironic look. 'Paul is a quiet, clever, intense scientist who had a glowing future ahead of him when he completed his thesis. He was engaged to a nice girl, and was in line for a substantial grant to carry on his research. Everything looked bright until trouble walked into his life in the tempting shape of Camilla Cavendish . . . is this ringing any bells yet?'

'No,' said Carey coldly, but her heart was sinking.

'In that case I'd better carry on with the story. Where was I? Oh, yes, your arrival on the scene. Well, Paul had never met anyone quite like you before, had he? He didn't stand a chance. I've never understood what you saw in him, though. Novelty, I suspect. And I dare say the fact that he was happily engaged added a little spice to the affair . . . am I right?'

Carey's eyes were a glacial grey, as cold as his. 'Get to the point.'

'Oh, I think you must remember the rest of the story by now,' said Drew. 'You picked on Paul, amused yourself for a while and then got bored. You didn't care that he'd left his fiancée for you or that he'd been so besotted with you that he'd forgotten about the final interview before the grant was awarded. Needless to say, it went to someone else, just as you did. You'd found someone more exciting and were ready to move on to pastures new. You couldn't be bothered with Paul then, could you? He was devastated. He'd lost the grant that would have enabled him to pursue a brilliant academic career, and he'd lost his fiancée . . . all for a worthless little tramp who made damned sure she left while the going was good!'

Carey's fists were clenched, her nails digging into her palms. How dared he talk about Camilla like that? How dared he? She wanted to hit him, to shout at him that he didn't know Camilla and that he wasn't fit to lick her boots. *She* knew Camilla. Her cousin believed in living life to the full, and, while the strait-laced—Carey foremost among them—might blink at her carefree attitude to men, Camilla had her own standards of morality that were, in their own way, strictly honest. She only ever got involved with men who were as free as she was. Many times Carey had heard her bemoan the fact that a particularly attractive man had turned out to be married or engaged and was therefore out of bounds, as it were. Camilla herself admitted that the reluctance stemmed from laziness as much as anything else, claiming that she simply couldn't be bothered to deal with the inevitable subterfuge and entanglements. If she had indeed been involved with Paul Jarman, Carey was absolutely certain that she hadn't known that he was engaged. Camilla might be easily bored, but she was never deliberately cruel.

Drew was watching her with narrowed green eyes. 'Well? Nothing to say for once?'

'Only that there are two sides to every story.'

He pounced on her words. 'So you *do* remember?'

'No,' she said clearly, looking him straight in the eye. 'Which means that it can't have been the passionate affair Paul has obviously made it out to be, or I certainly *would* have remembered.'

'Are you accusing him of making the whole thing up?'

Carey counted to ten and forced herself to sound coolly patient. 'I'm not accusing him of anything. I'm just *suggesting* that he's told you the story from his own point of view and that he may have my part in it out of perspective. I don't remember Paul, so all I can tell you is that C—that I,' she corrected herself hurriedly, hoping that Drew hadn't noticed the slip, 'have never knowingly had a relationship with a man who is already committed to another woman, so if Paul says I deliberately enticed him away from his fiancée then he's lying.'

'And you expect me to believe that?'

'Frankly, I don't care whether you believe me or not,' snapped Carey, losing her precarious hold on her temper. 'You're not even prepared to listen to any point of view other than your own. Has it ever occurred to you that your precious Paul might bear some responsibility for losing his fiancée? Why is it always the woman's fault? Paul ruined his own life, and I'm damned if I, or anyone else, should take the blame for him! Am I supposed to have dragged him off bodily? Was he incapable of saying no? Was it my job to remember his appointment for the grant interview? We're talking about a grown man, not a little boy.

'I suppose he blamed his fiancée for being too hard-hearted to take him back as well? Well, if I'd been her, I wouldn't have wanted anyone so spineless back either! He hasn't even got the guts to face me himself! Instead he's slunk off back to England and left you to fight his battles for him.' Incandescent with rage by now, Carey faced Drew with flashing eyes. 'I'm surprised you let him go and leave you alone with such a dangerous man-eater!'

Drew's mouth was a thin, angry line. 'Oh, I'm not afraid of succumbing to your charms, believe me!' he bit out. 'I'm not impressed by your fine show of righteous indignation, either. I like my women honest, and you, Miss Cavendish, don't qualify.'

Carey opened her mouth to protest hotly when she remembered just what she was doing there and shut it again. Travelling under a name that wasn't her own, pretending to be someone she wasn't didn't put her in a strong position when it came to arguments about honesty.

'Exactly!' mocked Drew, accurately interpreting the frustration at her own inability to defend herself in her glare, but unaware of its cause. 'You're in no position to preach about honesty, are you?'

Carey cursed her own weakness in promising Camilla that she wouldn't admit the truth in any circumstances. She had always had a straightforward, uncomplicated attitude that Camilla found annoyingly old-fashioned at times, and she had felt uneasy about this situation right from the start. It was her own fault for giving in to Camilla, Carey realised ruefully. There was no point in being like Paul Jarman and blaming everyone else for the impossible position she now found herself in. She had been just as capable as he of saying no firmly to Camilla, but she hadn't, and now she was just going to have to put up with consequences.

Drew had been watching the emotions struggling in her expression with a sardonic lift of his eyebrows. 'I shouldn't bother trying to think of a way to convince me that you're as innocent as you look. Even if I didn't know about Paul, there's something about you that just doesn't ring true. I don't trust you one little bit, Carey, and that's all the protection I need when it comes to resisting your undoubted appeal!'

'Believe me, you won't need any protection!' flared Carey. 'You're quite safe from me. I'd need to be pretty desperate before I tried to seduce *you*. Quite apart from anything else, you're just not my type!'

'Not malleable enough for you?' Drew pretended to consider while she clenched her fists and longed to haul out and thump him. 'I can understand that. You accused Paul of being weak, but that's just the kind of man you like, isn't it? You like someone you can push around, and you wouldn't be able to do that with me. It might be a new experience for you. It might even teach you a lesson.' He looked across at Carey's stormy face and a malicious light sprang into his eyes. 'Perhaps I'll try and seduce *you* instead.'

'You might as well spare yourself the effort,' said Carey, outraged. 'Do you really think I'd let myself be seduced by you? You've been arrogant, unpleasant, unreasonable and utterly detestable—I'm hardly likely to fall for *that* array of charms!'

'No?' Drew moved so quickly that he was beside her before she realised what was happening. Lifting her chin defiantly, she tried to hold her ground, but somehow she found herself backing away until she came up against the bamboo wall. 'That sounds remarkably like a challenge to me,' he told her softly.

Carey spread her fingers over the ridges in the wall as if for strength and swallowed. Her pulse was thundering in her ears and her throat felt so tight it was difficult to breathe, but she met his green gaze bravely, her own eyes huge and bright with alarm at the way her body was reacting to his closeness. 'It wasn't meant to be a challenge,' she said huskily. 'It was the truth.'

A speculative look came into Drew's eyes. Instinctively, reading its warning, Carey lifted her hands in a futile effort to push him away, but he caught her wrists, pinning them with insulting ease against the wall. 'The truth?' he echoed mockingly. 'I don't think you know how to tell the truth, Carey, but we'll see, won't we?'

She opened her mouth to protest, but it was too late. His lips came down on hers, and for Carey it was as if everything else ceased to exist. Time froze. She forgot the fraught journey and the fact that she hardly knew this hard, difficult man. She forgot Camilla and why she was here and the furious argument that had been taking place only moments ago. She forgot everything except

Drew and the piercing shock of recognition that over-whelmed her at the first touch of his mouth, as if her whole life had led up to this moment when she found herself in his arms.

Carey had an obscure, almost frightening sense of having come home at last after a long, arduous trip. It was absurd, of course. She could hardly have been further from home, isolated on a tiny tropical island with a hostile stranger who made no secret of the fact that he despised her. It was absurd to feel, when he took her in his arms, that she had never known what home was before.

Caught unawares by her own confused reaction, she forgot to struggle. Later, she thought that if he had been fierce or cruel she might have had some chance of re-sistance, but his mouth was warm and persuasive and she had no defences against a kiss that teased and tan-talised with the promise of delight, that solicited rather than demanded, intoxicating her senses and leaving her quivering with desire. Her body seemed to have ac-quired an instinctive life of its own, and her lips parted beneath his, returning his kiss with a sweetness that dis-solved the last memories of anger between them.

The kiss went on and on, neither of them capable of breaking its breathless, bewitching spell until, very slowly, Drew raised his head to look down into Carey's face with an unreadable expression. Still pinned help-lessly against the wall, she could only stare back up at him, her eyes dazed and dilated with wonder. For a moment, Drew stiffened and released her wrists as if he would have drawn away, but at the last second he changed his mind. With a muttered exclamation, he jerked her back into his arms.

This time his mouth was more demanding, more insistent, overwhelming that strange, unexpected sweetness in an irresistible tide of feeling. Carey clutched at Drew's shirt, her last anchor to reality as the intense, electrifying excitement that had smouldered between them since their first meeting burst at last into flames.

Drew tightened his arms about her, sliding his hands down her spine and up again to press her closer to deepen the kiss. Carey felt possessed, abandoned to a force far beyond her control as she clung to him, scorched and shaken by a blaze of response that threatened to consume her. She hadn't known it was possible to feel such sensation, to be gripped by such need, and when Drew's mouth left hers to trace a burning trail along her jaw and down her throat she tipped back her head and gave a breathless moan of inarticulate desire.

Her blood was pounding, her senses whirling in exquisite torment as Drew continued his devastating assault. His male-rough skin grazed tantalisingly against her neck, and she could feel him muttering into the shadowy hollows of her clavicle while his fingers undid the buttons of her demure white shirt, flicking them apart and brushing the material aside to allow him to explore the luminous ivory glow of her bare breasts. Carey gasped at the jolt of feeling that transfixed her as Drew's lips followed his hands, burning over her silken skin, savouring her softness, and her fingers, which had crept up his shirt to his shoulders, tightened convulsively in his dark hair in supplication.

'Please,' she gasped, pleading for him to stop this almost unendurable tide of sensation even as her body arched itself towards him in mute invitation to continue.

'Camilla...' Drew groaned, his breathing ragged as his mouth began to retrace its path to her lips once more, one arm around her back to hold her pliant body against him while the other caressed her breast possessively.

Camilla? Very gradually, the name filtered through the haze of arousal that swirled around Carey. When it did, it hit her with the force of a blow. Her eyes snapped open. Drew was pressing tiny kisses against her throat and over his shoulder she could see the kerosene lamp hissing and spluttering on the table, its white light throwing flickering shadows on the wall.

Camilla. Drew thought she was Camilla.

Hit by a wave of self-disgust, Carey jammed her hands against Drew's chest and pushed. He stiffened in surprise at finding the warm, yielding body in his arms suddenly transformed into struggling outrage, but released her immediately, stepping back without haste to watch her frantic, fumbling attempt to fasten her shirt once more.

'Well, Camilla?' he asked with a slightly twisted smile. 'Are you still ready to claim that you stand in no danger of being seduced by me?'

'More so than ever!' Carey was trembling, humiliated by the way her shaking fingers were having such trouble matching buttons to holes, but she met his eyes bravely, her own furious and glittering with self-loathing. 'And I've told you before, my name's Carey now.'

'Carey, Camilla...' Drew shrugged indifferently and Carey hated him for his ability to appear so unmoved by what had passed between them. 'You can change the name, but you can't change the woman underneath. Carey doesn't tell the truth any more than Camilla did.'

'I *am* telling you the truth!'

'Are you? You say you couldn't be seduced by me, but just now you were giving a very convincing demonstration of succumbing without even a token protest.'

Carey had at last managed to fasten her shirt. The buttons were all askew, but she shoved it angrily into her trousers anyhow, mortified by her own uninhibited behaviour and acutely grateful for the dim light that hid her burning face. Her cheeks felt as if they were on fire and she half expected to see them glowing through the shadows like a beacon. Had that really been her, clinging to him, moaning with pleasure, practically *begging* him to make love to her?

'For a man supposedly immune to my charms, you were giving a good impression of succumbing yourself!' she snapped, provoked into retaliation.

'Oh, I'm not denying that there's something very seductive about you,' said Drew, calmly reaching out to pull out her shirt from her trousers and proceeding to rebutton her shirt correctly with deft fingers. 'I can quite see why Paul was so besotted by you. The combination of a bewitchingly passionate woman beneath that deceptively cool exterior is effective enough to ensnare all but the most wary of men... but, fortunately for me, I'm very wary indeed of dishonest women, and I'm in no danger of forgetting that a liar lurks inside this inviting body.'

'In that case, why bother to kiss me at all?' Carey demanded furiously. She had been so staggered at the cool way he dealt with her buttons that at first she just stood there holding her breath while her senses spun at his nearness. It was only when she found herself noticing how infuriatingly steady his fingers were that she recovered and stepped abruptly back, slapping his hands away. How could he be so calm when her knees were weak and her heart still battered frantically against her chest, remembering his kisses, the feel of his lips against her breast, the hardness of his body pressed against hers?

'Why?' Drew shrugged. 'I'm a scientist. I wanted to know whether you were telling the truth or not.'

'So that . . . that *mauling* I just suffered was by way of being an *experiment*?' Carey's voice shook with fury and she wrapped her arms protectively across her chest so that Drew wouldn't guess that she still trembled from his touch.

'A very effective one, you must admit,' he said in a maddeningly reasonable tone that made Carey suck in her breath.

'I wouldn't describe it like that,' she said through her teeth.

'Come on, Carey, why not face the truth for once in your life? Your mouth said one thing but your body gave me quite a different answer!'

Carey looked at him stonily. 'You took me unawares.'

'I let you go as soon as you pushed me away, didn't I?'

It was true, although Carey had no intention of admitting it. She glared at him instead, her jaw working in frustration.

'You could have pushed me away at any time,' Drew went on relentlessly. 'But you didn't, did you? You might not like it very much now, but the truth is that at the time you enjoyed it.'

'You're not much of a scientist if your crummy "experiments" lead you to conclusions as wrong as that one!' Carey shook her hair angrily away from her face. 'I only hope your research is conducted a little more professionally, or Weatherill Willis is wasting its money sponsoring you!'

Drew eyed her stormy expression with a gleam of appreciation. 'Any experiment is valid if it teaches you something, but you can reassure your company that as far as the project goes my methods are completely orthodox. Fish are much more predictable creatures than women. At least I don't have to worry about them lying.' Turning away, he moved over to the table and adjusted the kerosene lamp, which was still hissing impotently.

The prosaic action infuriated Carey more than anything else. 'In that case, I'd appreciate it if you'd restrict your research to the marine world in future!' she said, tight-lipped. 'I don't feel like being the object of any more experiments!'

Drew glanced up from the lamp. Its glare threw his face into harsh relief, emphasising the angle of his cheekbones and the forceful lines of his nose and chin, but shadowing his eyes. 'Don't worry, they won't be necessary,' he said with an ironic look. 'I've already found out everything I need to know about you.'

Carey longed to haul out and hit him and for a moment the temptation to do just that was so overwhelming that she thought she was going to explode. Her eyes blazed at him, and her mouth was clamped tightly shut in an effort to keep the seething rage inside her. She was damned if she would give Drew Tarrant the satisfaction of arguing any longer!

'I'm going to bed,' she managed through set teeth. 'Alone!'

'You can have quarter of an hour,' said Drew, unmoved by her terrifying restraint. 'Then I'm going to bed too, whether you're ready or not. I've had a long day too, and I don't see why I should hang around waiting for you to get ready. I've got work to do tomorrow.'

Carey didn't deign to reply. With a last look of loathing, she swung on her heel and stalked through the bead curtain, wishing it were possible to slam it behind her. Her grand exit was spoilt, too, by the fact that she had forgotten that she would have to go past Drew again if she wanted a final wash.

He was sitting on the steps, his arms resting on his knees as he stared out to where the sea gleamed dully through the darkness. It had stopped raining at last, but the clouds blocked out any moonlight and Carey hesitated when she saw just how dark it looked over by the washing hut. She wished Drew hadn't told her about the snakes. She wished Drew hadn't done a lot of things.

Telling herself not to be so wet, Carey seized the kerosene lamp and marched outside. Drew needn't think she was worried about *anything*!

'Excuse me,' she said in freezing accents, and Drew moved over without a word to let her pass. Swinging the lamp in wide circles, she inspected every inch of the hut before she relaxed enough to put it down and brush her teeth.

'What were you looking for?' asked Drew as she made her way back. He stood up obligingly to let her back up the steps. 'There aren't any dangerous beasts around here.'

'That's a matter of opinion,' said Carey with a cold look.

Leaving the lamp on the table, she undressed quickly in the light filtering through the bead curtain and wrapped herself in a sarong. She was glad that Camilla had insisted on her bringing a sleeping-bag. At the time, she had thought it a waste of space, sure that it would be too hot to sleep beneath more than a sheet, but that was before she knew she would have to share a room with Drew Tarrant and would need all the protection she could get!

The camp bed was sturdy and surprisingly comfortable, but Carey found it impossible to relax. She lay with the sleeping-bag pulled defensively up to her chin and stared up at the ceiling. What a day! The terrifying flight through the storm clouds and that horrific boat journey already seemed remote, part of a life that was cut off from the present by Drew's kiss. Carey burned with the memory. His hands had been so hard, so sure, his mouth so warm and exciting.

What would have happened if he hadn't murmured Camilla's name and shattered the spell? In her heart of hearts, Carey knew that she would never have found the will to push him away otherwise. Would Drew himself have withdrawn, or would he have let the unexpected passion that had smouldered between them blaze to its natural conclusion? Would he be lying here now, running his hands over her skin, touching her and tasting her until she gasped with desire?

Carey turned over abruptly and banged the meagre pillow into a more comfortable shape. What had possessed her to start imagining *that*? The mere thought had been enough to set her pulse booming in her ears. There must be something wrong with her, she decided desperately. She had never acted like this before... but she had never met a man like Drew before, had never known that dizzying rush of excitement, that hunger, that need. The embraces she had shared with Giles had been chaste by comparison, Giles himself no more than a pallid imitation of what a man could be.

Carey thought of the years she and Giles had jogged steadily along together, each taking the other for granted. She had thought that she loved him, had thought for a time that companionship and security were the same as love, but when Giles had asked her to marry him she had been brought up short. The decision should have been obvious; Giles had certainly expected it to be obvious, but when the moment had come Carey hadn't found it obvious at all. All she knew was that she wanted something more than Giles could offer her. She wanted friendship and security, but she also wanted love.

Admit it, she told herself. You want a man to sweep you off your feet, a man to make you forget how calm and sensible you really are. You want to melt into his arms and thrill at his touch and shiver with excitement whenever he walks into the room.

You want him to make you feel the way Drew makes you feel, a little voice deep inside whispered to her.

Carey thrust the thought away. That wasn't what she wanted at all. She didn't even like the man, and he certainly didn't like her! His kisses might be exciting, but that wasn't *love*, any more than what she had felt for Giles had been love. She had been sad that her relationship with Giles had ended the way it had. He had been so certain that she would take their eventual marriage for granted that he had taken her refusal as a deliberate insult. Angry and aggrieved, he had refused to have anything more to do with her, and although Carey had been distressed at his bitter reaction she had also been conscious of a secret sense of relief. If she had married Giles, she would have been safe and comfortable, but she would always have wondered if there might not have been something more to life. Giles's attitude was awkward and embarrassing, but it had only convinced her that she had made the right decision. She wasn't going to make do with second-best, or compromise any more. If she couldn't find a perfect love, she wouldn't love at all.

Easy to decide, less easy to remember whenever she thought about the way Drew had kissed her, the way she had kissed him back...

Carey sighed and threw herself back to scowl up at the ceiling once more. She tried to close her mind to Drew, but it was impossible when his image seemed stamped on her brain. She had known him for less than twenty-four hours and already she could picture him with disturbing clarity: the cool, watchful face, the unnerving eyes, the firm mouth with its disquieting curve.

She knew exactly how he turned his head and how he screwed up his eyes against the rain. She saw him frowning, the cynical curl of his lip, the hard, suspicious stare and the way reluctant amusement bracketed his mouth. She remembered his smile and the reassuringly solid strength of his body. Most of all she remembered the intense delight of his kisses and how his hand had curved over her breast...

Stop it! Stop it! Stop thinking about it! Think about how unpleasant he was; think about how unfair he's been to Camilla; think about anything other than Drew's mouth and Drew's hands and how things might have been if I hadn't promised Camilla that I wouldn't tell the truth, she told herself sternly.

Next door, the kerosene lamp was abruptly extinguished, plunging the hut into darkness. Carey lay rigidly while Drew waited for his eyes to adjust. She had squeezed her eyes shut, feigning sleep, but it only seemed to heighten her other senses. The bead curtain rustled back into place as he stepped through and Carey, preternaturally aware of his every move, felt the room shrink around her. She could hear him undressing, the sound of a zip being undone, the muffled rustle of a shirt being pulled impatiently over his head, the protesting squeak of the camp bed as he lay down.

Carey found that she was holding her breath and let it out very carefully. Outside, a faint breeze whispered through the palm leaves and she could just hear the faint lap of the lagoon against the beach. She tried to concentrate on its restful sound, but when Drew shifted himself into a more comfortable position her heart leapt as if he had shouted.

It wasn't fair, she thought resentfully, listening to his steady, even breathing. Drew wasn't in the slightest bit disturbed by the thought that she was lying mere inches away from him. Why was she lying here vibrating like a tuning-fork? Turning surreptitiously on her side, she could just make out the line of his body and the faint sheen of his skin through the darkness. What would it be like to be able to reach across and let her hands drift over his sleek strength? The thought, once imagined, lodged like a burr in Carey's mind, and her fingers throbbed and tingled with the urge to discover for herself, an urge so strong that she had to clench her hands to keep them still.

Turning resolutely away, she lay with her back to Drew, aware of his every breath until he slipped effortlessly into sleep. It wasn't fair, she told herself again. *She* was the one who was exhausted by her long journey. She should have been asleep hours ago, but how could she sleep when her heart was galloping like the Charge of the Light Brigade and her pulse thundered in her ears? She would never be able to relax, not with Drew lying so close to her. It was all his fault. Carey pummelled her pillow into submission, wishing she could do the same with her memories, and lay back down with a heavy sigh. She might as well resign herself to a sleepless night.

CHAPTER FIVE

CAREY woke slowly. Blinking, still half asleep, she stared at the thin stripes of sunlight that squeezed through between the bamboo poles while her other senses tuned into her unfamiliar surroundings. Gradually, she became aware of the clean smell of wood and, somewhere in the distance, the unmistakable murmur of the sea. Then she realised that she was hot, and she struggled into a sitting position as reality came rushing back.

She was alone on Moonshadow Cay with Drew Tarrant.

The bed opposite hers was empty. Carey swallowed and clutched her sarong about her, remembering last night in a series of vivid, if jumbled snapshots: Drew's contemptuous expression, her own face white with fury, the feel of the bamboo digging into her back as he kissed her, the wild desire swamping the sweetness. Carey's mind veered away from remembering that peculiar sense of recognition she had felt. Really, the whole episode had been so unlike her. She must have been more tired than she thought.

Disentangling herself from the sleeping-bag, Carey secured her sarong firmly around her before padding cautiously over to the bead curtain. She parted it slightly and peered through, but to her relief there was no sign of Drew and she stepped out into the room. It all looked so different without the eerie, hissing glow of the kerosene lamp. Carey glanced at the place where Drew had pressed her against the wall, half expecting to see a scorch mark burnt into the bamboo, and the colour rising in her cheeks as she remembered the scene—the girl arching against him, her fingers tightening in his hair as she murmured with pleasure. In the bright light of day, it was hard to believe that the girl really had been her.

Carey averted her eyes. There was no point in pretending that it had just been a figment of her over-tired imagination, tempting as it was to think so. No, she would have to face up to facts. Last night she had behaved like the uninhibited seductress Drew had accused her of being. Somehow she was going to have to convince him that he had been wrong about her after all.

Where *was* Drew, anyway? The hut felt empty and silent without him. Carey wandered out on to the veranda and stopped dead, unprepared for the view that met her eyes. The bedraggled grey island she had glimpsed through the pouring rain had vanished so completely that she blinked, feeling as if she had stepped into quite a different world.

Beyond the shade, a curve of white sand glared in the dazzling light. It sloped gently down into the lagoon which shimmered like silk, deepening in colour from the palest glacier mint-green of the shallows to turquoise, shading into jade and then a bright, bright blue. Encircled by its protective reef, the lagoon was still and quiet, but in the distance, where the reef wall dropped sharply into deep water, the open sea surged softly, a darker, more intense blue, illuminated every now and then by a froth of brilliant white as a wave broke over the coral.

The colours were so vivid, the light so vibrant that they hurt Carey's eyes. Hardly aware of what she was doing, she went down the steps and across the clearing to curl her toes in the soft sand. The silence added to the air of unreality. The lagoon barely rippled against the sand.

There was no sign of Drew. The beach curved emptily off around the island, its fringe of coconut palms leaning out at absurd angles and splashing its pristine whiteness with tattered patches of shade.

Carey walked down to the lagoon. The water rocked up at her, warm and inviting and so clear that she could see the shadows of the tiny fish that darted away from her approach reflected on the white sand. With a sigh, she sank down, unwrapping her sarong as she went and luxuriating in the silky feel of the water against her skin. Camilla hadn't told her it would be like this.

Turning on her back, Carey floated across the lagoon and thought about Camilla. What was the truth of her relationship with Paul Jarman? According to Drew, she had been heartless and cruel, but then, he only had Paul's version of events. Carey was well aware that Camilla could be thoughtless and self-centred at times, but she was far from the bitch he had described. If only she could tell Drew the truth, she might be able to persuade him of that.

Drew.

Carey looked up at the sky. His image seemed to shimmer before her eyes, austere and angular and self-contained, with that intriguing hint of humour curling his mouth... Oh, God, she wished she hadn't remembered his mouth. Kicking up her legs, Carey dived beneath the water to wash away the memory, but it was hopeless.

She swam slowly towards the shore, wondering how she would face Drew after last night. Her sarong floated where she had left it, and she found her feet in the shallows while she wrapped the wet material around her with some difficulty. She would have to face him some time. She could hardly avoid him, after all. It would be hard to find excuses when they were the only two people on the island and had to spend the next fortnight sleeping a matter of inches apart. She couldn't leave, either. Even if there had been any way to get off the island, she couldn't run away before she'd had a chance to do the job she had promised to do. Camilla was relying on her, and Carey had no intention of letting her down, Drew Tarrant or no Drew Tarrant.

No, she was stuck here with him, so she would just have to make the best of it. She couldn't even claim that he hadn't warned her at the airport. He had given her the chance to change her mind, and she hadn't taken it. Somehow she would just have to convince Drew that her behaviour last night had been an aberration. From now on she would be cool and capable, calmly businesslike. She wouldn't allow him to provoke her or give him the slightest reason to suspect that she even remembered the way he had kissed her. Let him think that he had imagined the whole affair!

Buoyant with resolve, Carey wished she could face Drew there and then just to prove how little he affected her, but there was still no sign of him by the time she had dried herself and changed into a pair of knee-length shorts and a sleeveless cotton top. They made her feel neat and practical, and she wondered whether Drew would approve.

Not that she wanted his approval, Carey reminded herself hastily. She just wanted to impress on him that she was there on business and wasn't about to forget the fact again. Every few minutes she would go out on to the veranda to check whether Drew was on his way back to the hut to be impressed, until she began to irritate herself. Why did she care where he was, anyway?

Snatching up the dirty plates that had been left from last night, she washed them up in a frugal amount of water, and turned her attention to the hut, stacking away the plates, scouring the saucepans, cleaning the bench and wiping the table. When she came to the desk, she hesitated and glanced down at the papers Drew was obviously working on. They were covered with alarmingly sophisticated graphs, all of which might as well have been upside-down for all they meant to Carey. Books were piled on a makeshift shelf above the desk, and she tilted her head to one side to squint at the titles. Most were intimidatingly technical tomes, but a glossy blue cover caught her eye. *Beneath the Blue* . . . wasn't that the title of Drew's television series?

Carey riffled the pages of the book curiously, sniffing appreciatively at the expensive-smelling paper. The photographs were stunning, she noted enviously, and when she read the introduction she saw that Drew had paid a handsome tribute to all the photographers and sound men who had worked on the series in his introduction. Turning the book over in her hands, she ran her eye down the blurb on the back cover: 'Fascinating', 'Outstanding', 'Drew Tarrant opens up a whole new world to us with wit and wisdom', 'His scholarship is evident, but never intimidating—an original and absorbing account'. Carey raised her eyebrows. It had evidently been a much more successful series than she had realised.

Without thinking, she opened the back cover and found herself staring down at a photograph of Drew on the inside of the dust jacket. It was a head-and-shoulders shot, evidently taken on location somewhere for his hair was slightly ruffled by the wind. The camera had caught him unawares. He was looking relaxed, watching something behind the photographer, and a half-smile was curling his mouth. Carey looked at it, remembering how warm and exciting its touch had been, and something clenched into a hard knot inside her. Only last night, that mouth had explored hers, had drifted down her throat...

Banging the book shut, she shoved it back on the shelf. She was not going to think about that kiss any more!

Desperate to take her mind off the disturbing memories of last night, she seized a broom and began sweeping what seemed like several weeks of accumulated sand between the cracks in the floorboards. By the time Drew finally reappeared, she had worked off the worst of her frustration and was even humming to herself as she bent to sweep underneath the table.

He came up the steps so quietly that she didn't hear him at first. 'What are you doing?'

Drew's astonished voice behind her made Carey spin round with a gasp. He was standing in the doorway, his massive frame blocking out the light, watching her with an expression that was half amused, half speculative, and at the sight of him Carey felt her breath leak slowly out of her. She had remembered him so clearly, but even his photograph hadn't prepared her for the sheer impact of his presence or the impression he gave of a power kept under tight control. It left her feeling ridiculously flustered for a girl who had vowed to be cool, calm and collected, and she was furious with herself when the brush dropped from her fumbling hands.

'What does it look like?' she asked sharply to cover her nervousness, and bent to pick up the brush, horribly conscious of the tell-tale flush spreading over her cheeks.

'I just thought I'd clean up a bit, that's all. I presume you've no objection—or do you like living in a tip?'

'Not at all.' Drew moved into the room, letting the sunlight flood in behind him. 'I'm just surprised. I didn't know you were so domestic!'

'There are a lot of things you don't know about me,' said Carey, lifting her chin.

His unnervingly light eyes rested on her thoughtfully. 'So it seems.'

'Did you want something?' she asked coldly.

'I came back for a drink and to see whether you were awake,' he said, ignoring her frosty tone. 'You were fathoms-deep when I left.'

Carey didn't like the idea of Drew watching her while she slept. 'I was very tired.'

'Ah, yes. You had an eventful day yesterday, didn't you?'

'It's not an experience I'm anxious to repeat!' she snapped, insensibly annoyed by the lurking amusement in his eyes.

'What, none of it?'

He was definitely laughing at her! Carey pressed her lips together and glared at him. '*None* of it.'

Drew took the top off the kettle and peered inside to check that there was enough water before lighting the gas. 'Want a cup of tea?'

The abrupt change of subject caught Carey off balance. She longed to tell him that she didn't want anything, but that would just be childish. Besides, she was thirsty after all her exertions. 'Thank you,' she said stiffly after a moment, and Drew turned to lean against the bench in what was already a familiar position.

'You look better for a good night's sleep,' he said, observing her critically. She was still standing by the table, clutching the broom with both hands, her grey eyes bright with antagonism. Her skin was glowing and the straight brown hair, still damp from her swim, was tucked demurely behind her ears.

Carey felt herself grow hot under his eyes. Was he remembering that kiss? Was he thinking about how eagerly she had clung to him and kissed him back? She swallowed. Now was the time to show him that he had quite the wrong impression of her.

She propped the brush carefully against the wall and sat down at the table. 'I feel better,' she said, moistening her lips with the tip of her tongue. 'I—I wasn't myself last night.'

'Oh?' Drew raised an eyebrow. 'In what way?'

'Well, I don't normally carry on like that,' Carey said with difficulty. She couldn't look at him, but stared instead through the open doorway to the glittering turquoise lagoon.

'Like what?'

He wasn't going to make this easy for her, she realised with a flare of resentment that helped her meet his eyes with a hostile look. 'You know what I mean!'

'I'm not sure that I do,' said Drew with an assumption of polite interest. 'Surely you're not going to tell me that you've never kissed a man before?'

'No...I mean, yes...not like *that*.' Carey took a breath and started again. 'What I'm trying to say is that you took advantage of the fact that I was tired and angry, otherwise I would never have...responded like that.'

That disquieting smile was lurking around Drew's mouth again. 'If that's how you kiss when you're tired and angry, how do you kiss when you're in love?'

'That's not something you're ever likely to discover,' said Carey coldly, furious with herself for having wondered much the same thing about him.

'Careful, Carey, that sounds like another challenge!'

The shrill of the kettle interrupted Carey's blazing retort just in time. Clamping her mouth shut, she counted to ten. She was *not* going to let him provoke her. Hadn't she already decided that she was going to be cool and collected and let him be the one to feel awkward?

There was fat chance of *that*, she thought grumpily, watching the unhurried way Drew made the tea. Nothing seemed to unsettle him. Well, she would just have to make him think the same about her.

'Look, we got off on the wrong foot yesterday,' she said after a moment, proud of how even her voice was. 'I know you didn't want me here, but, now that I *am* here, don't you think we could put yesterday behind us and start again?'

Drew's eyes narrowed as he placed one of the enamel mugs on the table beside her and resumed his position at the bench, holding his own mug in one hand while he considered her. 'Do you really think it's as easy as that for me to forget all that I've heard about you from Paul—all of which has been borne out by my own experience of you, I might add?'

'I don't expect you to forget it,' said Carey, gritting her teeth and refusing to let go of her temper. 'You've made it very clear what you think about me, and I'm obviously not going to be able to change that. I'm not even going to try and change your mind. It just seems to me that the next two weeks would be a lot easier for both of us if you could just shelve your prejudices while I'm here and...well, start with a clean slate. We don't have to like each other, but we could at least be pleasant while we have to be together.'

There was a pause. 'So you want me to pretend that I met you for the first time this morning? That I know nothing about you?' Drew asked slowly.

'Why not?' She met his gaze squarely, her eyes grey and very clear. '*I'm* prepared to pretend that you haven't been unfailingly rude and unpleasant ever since I arrived, after all,' she pointed out in a crisp voice, and to her astonishment and the confusion of her heart, which seemed first to stop, then lurch into a series of clumsy somersaults before settling into an erratic hammering, Drew threw back his head and laughed.

'You don't lack nerve, I'll give you that!' Still grinning, he eyed her speculatively. 'All right. We'll call a truce.'

Carey was still trying to get her breath back after the disconcerting effect his laugh had had on her heart. 'Thank you,' she managed on a half-gasp.

'I suppose you want me to apologise for kissing you too?'

'Not unless you want to.' Carey cleared her throat. 'Personally, I'd prefer to draw a veil over the whole incident and forget it along with everything else that happened yesterday.'

A smile still lingered around Drew's mouth, and his eyes gleamed. 'I don't know that I'll find it that easy to forget that particular incident, will you?'

'I'm certainly going to do my best!' said Carey, but she avoided his eye.

Drew put down his mug and leant across to take her chin in one strong brown hand, forcing her face round so that she had to look up at him from her stool, her eyes wide with shock and a treacherous, shameful excitement. His fingers seemed to burn into her skin, and she was sure she could feel the exact imprint of his fingertips, every tiny ridge, every line.

'Do you think you'll succeed, Carey?' he asked softly, and his thumb caressed her cheek almost absently.

She was excruciatingly aware of him, of his pale eyes on her face and the hand holding her, not cruelly, but with an inescapable strength. She couldn't take her own eyes off his mouth, terrified that he was going to kiss her again, terrified that he wouldn't.

'Y-yes,' she whispered.

Drew released her chin, trailing his fingers up her cheek to tuck a wayward strand of hair back behind her ear. Carey's skin quivered beneath his touch and she swallowed. Her legs felt weak, but somehow she found the strength to push back the stool and stand up, stepping back from his hand.

'A . . . a truce, then?' she said unsteadily.

'A truce,' Drew agreed with that lurking smile. 'Shall we shake on it?'

Carey stared down at the hand he held out to her as if it might bite. She didn't want to touch him, didn't want to feel her senses leap in response or set her heart pounding, but when she glanced up at him she read the mockery in his eyes. He knew exactly what she was scared of. Tilting her chin, she took his hand.

His fingers closed round hers with an electric awareness that jolted up her arm and made her snatch her hand away instinctively. Cursing herself for her gaucheness, Carey bit her lip. What was it she had resolved? To be cool and calm and sensible—and here she was acting like a blushing schoolgirl every time he came near her! She really would have to pull herself together.

One thing was sure. *Drew's* hand wasn't tingling. His heart wasn't thumping against his ribs just because she had touched him. He was as cool as ever, draining his mug and setting it down on the bench.

'I'd better get back to work,' he said as if nothing had happened, and walked out of the door without a backward glance.

Nothing *had* happened, Carey reminded herself almost crossly. He had agreed to a truce and shaken her hand. Why was she getting herself in such a state? There was absolutely nothing to get in a state *about*!

'Nothing,' she said out loud as if to convince herself.

It didn't stop her stomach fluttering whenever she thought about his hand closing around hers, though. At last, in frustration, Carey thrust her feet into canvas shoes, grabbed her camera and marched down the steps. She wasn't going to waste any more time thinking about Drew! She was going to do the job she had promised Camilla she would do, she would stick it out for two weeks and then she would leave and never have to think about Drew Tarrant again.

The light was too intense to take successful photographs on the beach. After a moment's hesitation, she turned and followed a narrow path which led her across the cay through tangled, scrubby vegetation, so thick in parts that she glanced nervously from side to side, certain that the snakes Drew had mentioned so casually were lurking in the undergrowth. It was dank and gloomy in here, and Carey had to wave tiny biting flies frantically away from her face.

It was hard to imagine a luxury hotel in the middle of all this. Carey suspected that Emory Jones had only shown Camilla pictures of the beach and the lagoon, and took a few photographs of her own to prove to her cousin that there was a less than idyllic side to the island too.

The cay was long and narrow, and it didn't take her long to push her way through to the other side, where she found another burningly white beach. Shading her eyes, Carey squinted across the water. The reef was closer to the shore here, and beyond it she could see two tiny cays, just surfacing above the dark blue sea. They looked like cartoon desert islands, flat and sandy and empty except for two or three coconut trees, their fringed leaves drooping in the heat. She ought to be glad she hadn't ended up on an island that size with Drew!

Carey was hungry by the time she made it back to the hut. She hadn't had any breakfast, and when she glanced at her watch she saw that it was past midday. On an impulse, she threw together a salad, and packed it together with some bread and a bottle of water into a basket. What better way to show the spirit of their truce than by taking Drew some lunch? If she tried to avoid him, he would only guess how nervous he made her.

It was very hot on the beach, and Carey was glad of her hat. Camilla had shrieked in horror when Carey had dug it out of her wardrobe where it had lain since the last hot summer. 'You can't wear that!' she had protested, but Carey had insisted. She was fond of it, it kept the sun from the back of her neck, and besides, what did it matter what she looked like?

Camilla had never been able to understand that point of view. She spent hours getting ready every morning, and, as she pointed out, wouldn't be seen dead in a cotton hat, let alone one as battered as Carey's. Trying to imagine Camilla wearing it, Carey turned up the brim and chuckled to herself. Close as they were, there were some things over which she and her cousin were simply incompatible and clothes were one of them.

The lagoon rippled over her bare feet as she walked slowly along the shore, carrying her shoes in one hand and the basket in the other. She had walked all the way past the curved point at the far end of the cay before she saw Drew. He was out in the lagoon, pulling a mask and snorkel from his face as he waded back to shore. He was wearing a T-shirt over his swimming-trunks. It stuck to him like a second skin, and even from a distance Carey could see how it outlined the powerful chest and shoulders.

Drew didn't see her until he was almost at the beach. Carey had continued on a converging path, but when he looked up and saw her she found herself faltering to an uncertain halt. The idyllic scene seemed to focus on his lance-like figure, so that the blues and the greens and the bright light were no more than a backdrop to the sharply distinctive lines of his body. It was as if he was outlined against the unreal blue of the sky behind him.

In spite of her determination not to let him affect her, Carey felt the breath dry in her throat. Everything about him was so clear: his wet, dark hair, the faint red mark left by the mask, the way the water threw wavering reflections over his skin. Suddenly, ridiculously shy, she cleared her throat.

'I thought you might like some lunch.'

Drew stepped out of the water to join her on the beach, tugging the mask from round his neck. 'Is lunch one of the terms of the truce?'

'No,' said Carey, unaccountably ruffled by the way her eyes kept straying to his bare legs. They were long and tautly muscled and very brown, and drops of water still clung to the dark hairs. 'I was hungry and I thought you might be hungry too, but if you don't want anything I'm perfectly happy to go away again.'

The crease at the side of Drew's mouth deepened and his eyes lit with laughter. 'There's no need to be so touchy! As it happens, I *am* hungry. I was about to head back to the hut so you've saved me a trip.' He set off up the beach, leaving Carey to follow him, feeling as if she had been somehow ungracious.

'I suppose it *was* a sort of peace offering,' she admitted as she sank down into the cool shade of a palm.

'It's a very practical one anyway. I'm starving.' Drew's voice was muffled as, to Carey's consternation, he yanked his wet T-shirt up over his head. His chest was broad and strong, with a V of crisp hair arrowing down to his flat stomach. There wasn't an ounce of fat on him, Carey noticed before hastily averting her eyes. She picked up a piece of coconut husk and twirled it in her fingers, wishing she could stop imagining what it would be like to run her fingers over that sleek strength.

'No doubt you think that if anyone ought to be making a peace offering it's me,' Drew went on with another of his glinting looks.

Carey risked a glance at him. To her relief, he had found a dry shirt and shrugged it on, and was buttoning it up while he watched her with those disquietingly light eyes. The trouble was, it just reminded her of how he had dealt with the buttons on her own blouse last night, and a faint flush stained her cheeks at the memory. Was that what he thought she wanted an apology for?

'No,' she said and forced herself to meet his gaze. The light caught her eyes, turning them almost silver beneath the brim of her hat. 'I've told you, you don't need to apologise for anything. We agreed that we would start afresh.'

'So we did.' Drew's fingers stilled on the last button as he looked down into her face, framed by the soft battered hat. His smile was rather twisted and he hesitated, as if tempted to say something further, but in the end he only turned away to spread his wet T-shirt out to dry. 'So we did.'

Outside the patch of shade where they sat, the sun glared down on the sand and bounced off the water. Carey felt isolated with Drew in a small circle of coolness, and she was very conscious of him lounging beside her as they shared a companionable lunch. Drew was flatteringly impressed by the salad.

'I don't usually bother much with lunch. This makes a nice change from tinned tuna and crackers.'

Carey laughed. 'I'd have thought you'd had enough of fish!'

'There are times when I'd be grateful if I never saw a fish again,' Drew admitted with a grin, helping himself to some more salad. 'It's a matter of practicality, really. Twice a year we have a team of volunteers who come and help take data readings, and when they take it in turns to cook the food really improves, but when Paul and I are here together we don't have the time to worry about cooking and cleaning. We rely on tins and things that are quick and easy...it gets a bit monotonous at times, but you get used to it after a while.'

'It doesn't sound very healthy,' said Carey disapprovingly, and then she sighed as her eyes strayed out to the lagoon shimmering in the midday heat. 'Still, I don't suppose you care what you eat when you're living in a place like this.' A wave broke over the reef with a brilliant splash of white. 'It's beautiful,' she said softly, leaning forward to link her arms around her knees. She glanced down at Drew. 'Do you ever get used to it?'

Drew wasn't looking at the view. He was stretched out beside her, watching her face with a curious expression.

'Sometimes it feels so much like home that perhaps I do take it for granted that I can just step outside and find a deserted beach on my doorstep, but I never get used to the beauty of the reef itself.' He lay back, resting his head on his hands, and looked up through the elegantly drooping palm leaves. 'It makes all of this look dull.'

'*Dull*?'

'It's a different world down there,' Drew tried to explain. 'You've never seen colours like there are on a reef. The coral's spectacular enough in itself, and then you've got every shape and size of fish. Some of them are incredibly coloured and patterned, some of them are just bizarre.' The austere features had softened with enthusiasm. 'And none of them is still. When you're diving off the reef, sometimes it's like being in a kaleidoscope of colour and movement——' He broke off with a half-embarrassed laugh. 'That doesn't sound very scientific, I know, but there's so much activity down there that it's almost disorientating to surface and find the beach here so still and empty.'

'It sounds wonderful,' said Carey wistfully, looking out across the lagoon and trying to imagine the scene that roused this implacably guarded man to such enthusiasm. Would he ever look that way about a woman?

There was a tiny pause. 'You could see for yourself,' said Drew carefully. 'I could take you out with me tomorrow morning... if you wanted to come.'

'Oh, I'd love to!' Carey turned to him impulsively, her eyes alight. 'Could I really come?' Her face fell as a thought struck her. 'You're not diving, are you? I've never done that.'

'I'll just be snorkelling again tomorrow. Presumably you've done that?'

'Carey shook her head. 'I've never been anywhere like this before.'

'Never?' Drew propped himself on one elbow and stared at her. 'I thought you were a great traveller.'

Camilla was, of course. Carey cursed herself for such an obvious mistake. 'I am,' she said carefully, 'but I've always found just lying on a beach rather boring. I like mountains and hills and wide open spaces where you can walk and walk.' Her eyes were soft as she remembered Yorkshire and the moors and dales she loved so much. 'I'd never have thought of coming to a place like this, but now I'm here . . . well, it's different from what I expected. It's so clean and quiet. I never dreamt it would be this beautiful.'

'It won't be clean and quiet any more if you build a resort here,' said Drew, the hard edge back in his voice. 'And if you don't like beaches, why are you so keen on the idea?'

Carey bit her lip. 'I'm *not* keen. I've just been sent out here to assess the potential for a resort and make a report. It isn't up to me.' That was true enough, after all, but Drew was unimpressed.

'That wasn't the impression we received from your messages. It was all "I" this and "I" that . . . "my idea", "my ambition", "my decision". All very self-important!'

Carey suppressed a sigh. She might have known! Camilla was never one to miss the opportunity to inflate her own importance. Not for the first time over the past couple of days, she wished her cousin was a quiet little homebody who wouldn't say boo to a goose . . . but then she wouldn't be Camilla.

'I'm sorry if my messages read rather tactlessly,' she said eventually. 'They obviously gave you a very misleading impression of me.'

'It didn't seem misleading to Paul. It seemed all too familiar!'

If Paul had known Camilla, Carey could believe it! A tiny smile tugged at the corner of her mouth. 'Perhaps I've changed since Paul knew me,' she suggested.

Drew was watching her smile suspiciously. 'Have you changed enough to realise that the very idea of a resort here is criminally irresponsible?'

'That's rather an exaggeration, surely?'

'Is it? Have you *thought* about what a resort would mean? This quiet beach you were admiring so much a few seconds ago would be full of people. The lagoon would be criss-crossed with jet-skis and people water-skiing. Do you think you'd like it so much then?'

'It doesn't have to be like that,' Carey protested. 'You just don't like the idea of not having it all to yourself any more!'

'Of course I don't!' Drew's eyes were very cold once more. 'How much research would we be able to do with holiday-makers frisking all around us? Not that there would be much left *to* research by the time they'd finished building a hotel. Everything would have to brought in by boat, even when it was completed. It would be like running a motorway through the reef. It can't stand up to that sort of pollution; after a while the coral just dies. Do you really want to be responsible for that?'

'Do *you* want to be responsible for depriving Emory Jones of the right to do what he wants with his island?' Carey retorted. 'You can't blame him for wanting to make a living.'

'Emory isn't exactly struggling to make a living,' said Drew drily. 'He's one of the richest men in Belize. Property development is just the latest in a series of lucrative pies he's got his sticky fingers stuck into, but I don't blame him for that. No, I blame people like you.'

Carey's chin came up in surprise. 'What do you mean?'

'It's comfortable for you to pass the buck on to Emory and his kind, but you're just using them. They make a little money, but it's a tiny fraction compared to how much a company like Weatherill Willis rakes in. You sit in your smart city offices and think up schemes like this, so intent on the lure of profit that you never give a thought to the consequences of what you do!'

'That's not fair!'

'No, I don't think it's fair either,' said Drew, deliberately misunderstanding.

Light green eyes clashed with grey, before Carey sighed. It had all been going so well and now they were squabbling again! 'I thought we'd agreed on a truce?'

Drew's glare faded and he grinned reluctantly. 'It's too hot to argue anyway. It's too hot to do anything.' He settled himself back in the shade and, reaching for a hat, tipped it over his face. 'Siesta time, I think.'

CHAPTER SIX

CAREY envied Drew his ability to ignore her so utterly. For a while she sat, hugging her knees, looking out to sea and trying not to think about the man who lay, relaxed and comfortable, beside her. Every now and then a cat's-paw of wind would shiver across the lagoon and rustle the branches overhead, letting the sunshine flicker across the shade for an instant before they swayed back into place.

It was very quiet. Carey glanced down at Drew. His head rested on his hands and the hat hid all his face except for the decisive line of his jaw and that long, firm mouth. Just looking at it gave Carey a strange feeling in the pit of her stomach.

How would Drew react if she leant across and touched her lips to the corner where his smile began?

The thought was so terrifyingly tempting that Carey linked her hands tightly together around her knees and stared fiercely down at them. When she risked another peep at Drew, she saw that his chest was rising and falling steadily. He was asleep. If only his mouth would fall open, or he would snore... anything to remind her that she really rather disliked him and that this feeling twitching and twisting and tightening uncomfortably inside her had absolutely nothing to do with desire.

Deciding that it would be easier if she stopped looking at him, Carey lay back cautiously and closed her eyes. The sand was soft and cool, and she wriggled her shoulders into a comfortable little hollow. Yes, this was much easier. If she concentrated hard enough on the insides of her eyelids she might even forget that Drew was there at all.

The hypnotic sigh and ripple of the lagoon soon had its effect. Carey drifted off into sleep and dreamt about Drew. They were swimming in the lagoon and he was smiling at her, and as he swam towards her they suddenly found themselves, in the manner of dreams, back on the beach. Drew was bending over her, lowering his head to kiss her, and Carey was smiling...

She was still smiling as her eyes opened languorously, and it seemed entirely naturally to find herself looking up into Drew's face. His eyes reminded her of the lagoon; they could look cool and clear and green, but sometimes they could deepen and darken, like now, with an expression which was hard to interpret but which made Carey's sleepy smile fade into a slow, steady thump of desire.

He was propped up on one elbow, leaning over her as in her dream. For a long, long moment they just stared into each other's eyes while behind them the lagoon sighed unnoticed. Carey couldn't have moved if she had tried.

Drew lifted his hand to trace the delicate line of her cheek. 'When you smile like that, it's very hard to remember who you are,' he said softly. 'What were you smiling about?'

'I was dreaming.' Carey's voice was barely a whisper.

'What about?' His finger drifted along her jaw. It was the lightest of touches, but it lit a trembling flame deep inside her, a flame that was fanned by the hazy excitement of his body so tantalisingly close.

'I can't remember,' she whispered again, but she did. She remembered only too clearly, so clearly that she was sure Drew could read the truth in her eyes.

'Was it this?' His hand slid back to spread her hair through his fingers as his gaze moved lingeringly over her face, and then, slowly, very slowly, agonisingly slowly, he bent his head. Carey's blood was pounding with a treacherous anticipation that held her breathless and incapable of pushing him away, and when he stopped, his lips almost but not quite touching hers, she was unable to prevent her eyes darkening with disappointment. 'Was it this?' he breathed against her mouth, and Carey gave a tiny sigh of release that might have meant 'yes' as his lips found hers at last.

His mouth was gentle, almost tender, but irresistibly persuasive, and Carey yielded beneath it, parting her lips to the delicious quest of his tongue, returning his kiss with a gathering need as the flame inside her leapt and burned, higher and higher until neither of them could control it. Drew had braced himself above her but as the kiss deepened he sank down on to her, pressing her back into the sand with the weight of his body. Carey's fingers slid along his forearms, loving the feel of the rough hairs beneath her palms before creeping up over the iron biceps and on to link around his neck and pull him closer.

It was Drew who broke the kiss with difficulty, burning kisses over her cheek to the wildly beating pulse below her ear, teasing her lobe with his tongue. 'Is that what you were dreaming about?' he murmured, and Carey felt him smile against her skin.

The whirling magic vanished so suddenly that Carey felt as if she had been on a roundabout that had stopped with a sickening jar, jolting the sea and the sky and the

branches overhead back into place and leaving her
shocked and disorientated. Her hands fell from his neck,
and she struggled beneath him, but his body held her
pinned to the sand.

'No!'

Drew's eyes were alight with laughter and something
else as he looked down into her stormy face. 'No? Are
you sure?'

'Of course I'm sure!' Carey finally managed to heave
him off, although it was only because he let her. She
struggled to her feet, panting. 'Why should I waste my
time dreaming about *you*?'

'No reason at all—particularly not when you can have
the reality,' said Drew, amused and so patently uncon-
vinced by her outrage that Carey stood over him
clenching and unclenching her fists with fury. 'Or are
you going to claim I took you unawares again?'

'I was half asleep!'

'You didn't seem very sleepy to me,' he commented,
getting easily to his feet. 'I'd have said that you were
positively stimulated!'

'Well, you'd have been wrong!' Carey shouted and
then gasped as Drew grabbed hold of her and yanked
her back against him. 'Let me go!'

He smiled grimly. 'Not until you admit that you're
lying as usual! I can tell when a woman's half asleep in
my arms, and you, Carey, were wide awake—awake and
aware and very responsive!'

Carey jammed her hands against his chest and tried
to shove him away, but he was rock-hard and un-
yielding, and when she abandoned that attempt to beat
her fists against him he only tightened his iron grip. 'Let
go of me!' she demanded furiously.

'Tell the truth first!' Relentlessly, Drew bore her backwards until she came up against the trunk of a palm. Its ridges dug painfully into her back. 'Go on, admit that you knew exactly what you were doing and I'll let you go.'

'No!' Carey turned her face stubbornly aside, but he put his hard palm flat against her cheek and pulled it back to face him. 'Don't!' she said in a more uncertain voice, afraid that he would kiss her again. She would never be able to control herself if he did. 'Don't,' she whispered again.

'Admit it.'

Carey stared angrily up into his implacable face, her jaw working in frustration. 'All right!' she snapped at last. 'I'll say I was awake all the time, if that will make you happy!'

'And responsive?'

'And responsive,' she said between clenched teeth. 'Now, will you please let me go?'

'Certainly.' Drew released her and Carey rubbed her sore back resentfully as he stepped away with a wicked grin. 'When are you going to learn that it'll be much easier if you just tell the truth in the first place?'

Carey didn't trust herself to speak. Instead, she snatched up her hat and swung it furiously against a tree to remove the sand, wishing she could do the same with Drew Tarrant. Glancing up, she saw that he was watching her with unmistakable amusement. So he thought she was funny, did he?

'I hate you!' she said childishly, and, jamming her hat on her head, she turned and ran away along the beach towards the safety of the hut.

She was still sulking that evening when Drew came in. The light was fading rapidly and all over the island hidden insects were warming up for an evening chorus of shrill whirrs and clicks. She had taken out some of her bad humour in preparing supper, savagely chopping onions and slicing peppers with ferocious concentration.

Drew didn't appear to notice the way she was banging pots around. He dropped the picnic basket and the shoes Carey had left behind on the floor, and helped himself to a beer from the small solar-powered fridge. 'Do you want one?'

'No, thank you,' said Carey frigidly. He might at least have the grace to look embarrassed about the scene this afternoon!

Evidently, Drew didn't feel in the least bit embarrassed. He pulled out a stool and sat down at the table to drink his beer straight from the bottle, unperturbed by her frosty silence.

'What have you been doing this afternoon?'

Carey crashed a saucepan down on to the gas ring. 'What do you care?'

'I was just making polite conversation.' The smile in his voice only made Carey angrier.

'You needn't bother!'

'I thought we agreed on a truce?'

'It's a pity you didn't remember that this afternoon!' she snapped, picking up the knife and attacking some tomatoes. 'And don't pretend you don't know what I mean!'

'I was making love, not war,' Drew said in an infuriatingly reasonable voice, but his eyes were dancing with amusement. 'I thought you'd approve. You were the one who suggested an end to armed hostilities after all!'

'I didn't suggest that you kiss me like that!'

'How would you like me to kiss you?' he asked, looking at her over the rim of his beer.

Carey's fingers tightened round her knife. 'I don't want you to kiss me at all!'

'In that case you'll have to try not to respond quite so passionately next time,' said Drew.

'There isn't going to be a next time,' she told him, her voice shaking with fury. 'I thought it would be easier if we both tried to behave in a civilised way while I was here, but it's not going to work if you're going to be unfair.'

Drew assumed an innocent expression. 'Unfair? How have I been unfair?'

'It was unfair of you to kiss me...like *that*,' said Carey, provoked.

'And I suppose it was unfair of me to let you kiss me back?'

A flush spread up her cheeks and she turned her back on him. 'And you didn't need to bully me like that afterwards,' she said, ignoring his question.

'You didn't like it, did you?'

'Of course I didn't!'

Drew finished his beer and stood up. 'What you don't like, Carey, is finding someone you can't push around for once. It's a new experience for you, isn't it? Paul might find it rather ironic to hear you complaining about unfairness!'

Carey put the knife down and turned back to face him. 'I thought we were going to start afresh? You said you'd forget about Paul for the next two week.'

'How can I forget when you keep reminding me just how dishonest you can be? I look in those clear, lovely eyes of yours and I almost believe that you're as innocent as you seem, and then you deny the obvious. I might be able to forget about Paul when you start telling the truth.' He dropped his empty bottle into a crate and headed for the door. 'I'm prepared to be "civilised", as you put it, but to my mind being civilised means being honest, so, if you want me to put my preconceptions about you to one side, don't whine to me about fairness. It's up to you.' He turned for the steps. 'You can think about it while I have a shower.'

Carey scraped the rest of the vegetables into the pan and adjusted the flame. How could she be honest with Drew when her very presence here was a lie? She felt oddly deflated. Her anger had kept her buoyed up all afternoon, but she should have been angry with herself, not with Drew. He was right. She had responded to his kisses eagerly, even demandingly, and then blamed him, because it was easier than admitting how little control she had over her own body.

They were scrupulously polite to each other over the meal, by tacit consent making no reference to the furious argument that had gone before. Drew had changed into a soft khaki shirt, its sleeves rolled up above his wrists, and cotton trousers. His damp hair was slicked down to his head.

'This is good,' he said in some surprise when he tasted the fresh vegetable sauce Carey had made to go with some pasta. 'First the salad, now this...I hadn't realised you were such an accomplished cook.'

'I like cooking,' said Carey, embarrassed by his praise of such a basic dish. 'I like all sorts of boring things like cooking and ironing and gardening. I'll spend hours happily weeding or cleaning the kitchen. Ca—my *cousin*,' she corrected herself quickly, 'says I'm an obsessive. She thinks I'm crazy to waste my time on chores like that, but I always end up feeling rather embarrassed by it.'

Drew raised an eyebrow. 'Why should you?'

'Oh, I don't know.' Carey was beginning to wish she hadn't told him as much as she had. 'I suppose I think I should be doing something more exciting.'

'In the spirit of our truce, I won't make the obvious comment,' said Drew with a dry look. 'But I will admit that I'm surprised. Camilla Cavendish, the perfect wife!'

Carey lifted her chin. 'There's more to being a wife than acting as some man's housekeeper. Marriage should be a partnership based on love and friendship, not convenience.'

'I couldn't agree more, but it doesn't often work out that way, does it?'

There was no mistaking the bitter edge in Drew's voice, and Carey glanced at him curiously. 'It can do.'

'Not in my experience. I've seen too many marriages where one partner is just used by the other, and dropped as soon as that usefulness ceases.'

'Is that why you're not married?' asked Carey after a moment's hesitation, and he shrugged.

'One of the reasons. I learnt my lesson about women the hard way, and the experience was enough to make me decide that I would never get married unless I could find a completely honest woman...and I certainly haven't found one yet.' He glanced at Carey and then away. 'Besides,' he went on, making an effort to lighten his tone, 'my life at the moment is unlikely to appeal to a wife. Either she'd have to put up with my being away for six months every year, or she'd have to be prepared to live in primitive conditions on a desert island with nothing to do all day. It would be all right for a week or so, but six months...you wouldn't like it, would you?'

Carey reached to gently stop a moth blundering into the kerosene lamp. 'I would if I loved you enough,' she said without thinking. It was only when she looked across at Drew once more that she heard what she had said, and a flood of colour swept up her throat. 'I meant . . . hypothetically . . .' She trailed off awkwardly.

There was a silence. To Carey it seemed to strum with tension, drowning out the whirring insects and the rustling palms.

'You seem to have a surprisingly romantic view of marriage,' said Drew after a moment. 'How come you're still single if you feel like that?'

Carey fiddled with the fork on her empty plate, remembering Giles and how when the chance of marriage had come she had turned it down. 'I haven't met anyone I loved enough,' she said honestly.

'Yet,' Drew added for her. His voice sounded strange and she raised her eyes slowly to meet his.

'Yet,' she agreed.

The lamp hissed quietly between them. 'So you've never even considered marrying anyone?' he asked as if the words were forced out of him.

'I did think about it once,' said Carey, pushing her plate aside and resting her folded arms on the table. 'I went out with Giles for nearly three years. For a time I did think I was in love with him, but it was just habit . . . convenience, as you said. It was a small town and we were fond of each other and there wasn't really anybody else. We just drifted along. Then he asked me to marry him and I suddenly imagined what the rest of my life would be like if I did. That's when I knew that I didn't really love him.' She looked down at her hands. 'I wanted something more,' she said in a low voice. 'I wanted to be loved and cherished, not taken for granted. I wanted a friend, of course, but I also wanted someone to make me feel like a woman——'

Carey broke off. Why was she telling Drew all this? She risked a glance across at him. His eyes were fixed on her face, but his expression was unreadable. 'I suppose you might say that I was using Giles, but it didn't feel like that at the time. I was as surprised as he was to discover that we weren't in love at all.'

'And how did this Giles react to the fact that after three years you'd suddenly decided you'd had enough?' asked Drew in a hard voice, obviously thinking of Paul and Camilla.

Carey's eyes were very direct. 'He went out and got engaged to someone else.'

'It must have been a change for you to be the one feeling rejected,' he commented without sympathy. 'I don't suppose you liked that at all.'

'I didn't mind,' said Carey evenly. 'I hope it means he's realised that we would both have been making a mistake if I'd agreed to marry him. He was furious at the time.' She grimaced at the memory of the painful scene. 'The only thing I don't like is the fact that he still won't talk to me or acknowledge me, even though he's found someone else. I wouldn't have said that he was capable of bearing such a grudge, but now I wonder if I ever knew him properly at all. I was only trying to be honest with him,' she said with another glance at Drew. 'I thought we were friends, and that we could stay friends, no matter what happened.'

'You're not the kind of girl men are content to be just friends with.'

There was an odd note in Drew's voice. Carey stared at him across the kerosene glare. His expression was quite unreadable, but for some reason she suddenly found herself growing hot.

Getting abruptly to her feet, she carried her plate across to the bench where another lamp hung from the wall. What on earth had possessed her to tell Drew about Giles and her own muddled desires? He was too cynical even to begin to understand.

Embarrassed, unwilling to look at him, she made a great show of clearing up. Behind her, she heard Drew's stool scrape across the wooden boards. He brought his plate across to her and set it down on the bench.

'Looks like you've got a touch of sunburn there,' he said, brushing his fingers over a red patch on her shoulder.

Carey reacted as if he had stung her, jerking her arm away from the electric impact of his touch. Drew raised an eyebrow.

'Is it sore, or are you just tense?'

She flushed. An enamel plate slipped between her fumbling fingers and crashed tinnily to the floor, and she bit her lip as she bent to pick it up. 'It's a bit sore, that's all.' She had been careful to put on sun-cream before she went out, but she seemed to have missed that thin strip on her shoulder. It *was* a bit sore, but that wasn't why she had leapt away from him. She knew it, and so did Drew. His eyes mocked her.

'You need to be careful of the sun.'

'We do see the sun occasionally in Yorkshire,' she snapped. I don't need you to tell me how careful I need to be!'

Drew ignored that. 'Yorkshire? I thought you lived in London?'

'I do,' said Carey quickly. It was all too easy to slip up when she lost her temper, and Drew didn't miss anything! 'I grew up in Yorkshire,' she explained. 'I go back there as often as I can. I . . . I still think of it as home.'

'So you're just a simple country girl at heart?' he said with an ironic look.

A smile touched the corners of her mouth as she thought of Camilla, the ultimate town mouse, who shuddered at Carey's quiet country existence. 'You could say that.'

'What's so amusing?' asked Drew suspiciously and Carey turned away to put the kettle on for the washing-up. His eyes were too sharp for comfort. 'Nothing,' she said. 'Nothing at all.'

It seemed uncomfortably intimate to be washing up while Drew stood beside her to dry the plates and put them away. They might have been a happily married couple, were it not for the tension that twanged between them. Carey told herself she was being ridiculous, that she was imagining things. Drew wasn't doing anything. He wasn't even touching her. He was just standing there, drying the plates, the shadows from the lamp on the wall playing over his face. What was there in that to twist her stomach or make her heart boom and thump with awareness?

'I . . . I think I'll go to bed,' she said when they had finished.

She felt stupidly jumpy as she walked back from the wash-house. She was climbing the steps as Drew came out on to the veranda, and, terrified of brushing against him, she edged around him to the doorway. Before she got there, he put out an arm, leaning against the door-jamb to block her way.

'Why are you so nervous?' he asked softly.

Carey stopped short. His arm was as solid and un-yielding as an iron bar and she knew from previous experience that there was no point in trying to push past. Touching her hair behind her ears in an unconsciously defensive gesture, she moistened her lips. 'I'm not nervous.'

'Then why do you shy away every time I come near you? You're like the proverbial cat on a hot tin roof!'

Carey gritted her teeth. 'Look, I am *not* nervous!'

'I think you are.' Drew's free hand slid up her bare arm. 'I think you're afraid I'm going to kiss you again.'

'I hope you're going to reassure me that if that *were* the case I would have absolutely nothing to be afraid of?' she said bravely, even though she was sure he must be able to feel her skin quivering beneath his fingers.

'I'm making no promises,' said Drew, and his smile glinted through the darkness. 'But if it makes you feel any better, I'm not going to kiss you...not now, anyway.'

'Oh.' Carey was horrified to hear the disappointment in her voice. She cleared her throat. 'Good,' she said more firmly. 'Well, now that we've cleared that up, perhaps you would let me through?'

Drew's arm dropped from the door and he stood back with a mock-bow. 'I'll be the perfect gentleman and take myself off for a walk while you get ready for bed.'

She watched him walk across the clearing and out into the moonlight. Through the trees, she could see the lagoon gleaming like silver. It would be cool and quiet on the beach. It would be nice to walk down there after him, to stand with him in the darkness listening to the sea, to lean against his solid strength and feel the sand cool and soft beneath her bare feet...

Carey turned abruptly and went into the hut. In spite of the chinks in the walls, the bedroom was airless and claustrophobic and the thought of the beach was more tempting than ever. Undressing quickly, Carey threw herself down on her bed and closed her eyes. She had never felt less like sleep. The image of the moonlit beach spun in her mind, beckoning her outside, but she forced herself to lie still. Drew would only think that she had gone out to wait for him, and Carey's pride recoiled at the thought. Better by far to be hot and restless than down on the beach with Drew where pride would count for nothing next to the breathless excitement of his touch.

'Come on, Carey, wake up!' A hand was shaking her shoulder and Carey surfaced groggily.

'Wh-what's the matter?'

Drew was squatting beside her camp bed, but he sat back on his heels when he saw her eyes blink open with difficulty. 'I thought you wanted to go snorkelling?'

'Snorkelling...?' Completely disorientated, Carey struggled up, clutching her sarong about her, and groped on the floor for her watch. She squinted blearily at it. 'It's only half-past six!'

'I want to make an early start,' said Drew briskly. 'If we leave it too late, you'll get badly burnt... as I'm sure you know from your experience of the Yorkshire sun!'

'Isn't it a little early for sarcasm?' said Carey, with an attempt at dignity. She felt at a distinct disadvantage, still tousled and blinking with sleep, while Drew looked revoltingly crisp and efficient and awake.

He grinned at her affronted expression. 'Are you always this grumpy when you wake up?'

'I don't usually get woken up at the crack of dawn!' she said a little sulkily.

'I've brought you some tea,' he said, 'but I'll take it away again if you don't want to come. You can go back to sleep.'

'I won't be able to go back to sleep now,' Carey grumbled, taking the mug from him and wishing he wouldn't smile like that this early in the morning. It was bad for her heart.

Drew straightened. 'Does that mean you *do* want to come?'

'I might as well,' she said ungraciously.

'In that case, you'd better get a move on.' Drew moved to the door. 'You'll need a T-shirt over your swimsuit to protect your back and plenty of sun-cream. I'm going to take the kit down to the boat, and if you're not there in ten minutes I'm going without you!'

Carey's grumpy sleepiness dissolved as she gulped at her tea and splashed water over her face. Stepping into a plain black swimsuit, and pulling on a white T-shirt as instructed, she paused only to grab some fruit from the basket on the bench before running down to the jetty with a minute to spare. She wouldn't put it past Drew to leave early just to teach her a lesson, and now that she was awake she had discovered just how much she wanted to go with him.

But Drew hadn't left. He was sitting in the boat, checking the snorkelling equipment piled around his feet. He was wearing a faded blue polo shirt over his trunks and the battered hat was pushed back on his head. He glanced up as Carey ran breathlessly along the jetty.

'What's the panic?'

'You said you'd go if I wasn't here in time!'

Slow amusement lit Drew's eyes and a smile bracketed his mouth. 'I had no idea you took my words so much to heart, Carey. Did you imagine me sitting here checking my stop-watch?'

'It wouldn't have surprised me at all!' snapped Carey, feeling rather foolish.

Drew gave another of those heart-shaking grins that had such a disturbing effect on her breathing. 'Comfort yourself that you've surprised *me* instead! When I left you, you didn't seem at all keen on the idea of going snorkelling. I certainly wasn't expecting you to come rushing down here in case I left without you!'

'Oh, well . . .' Carey avoided his eyes, scuffing her toes on the jetty. 'I'm not very good first thing in the morning.'

'I noticed!'

'I like to wake up slowly,' she explained, not really knowing why she wanted him to understand that she wasn't always that grumpy.

'The way you did yesterday afternoon?'

Drew's eyes were very green, very bright in his tanned face, the fringe of dark, almost sooty eyelashes unnaturally clear in the morning light. Carey was sure she could see every crease around his eyes. Yesterday afternoon. The memories she had tried so hard to suppress washed over her: her fingers drifting up his arms, the taste of his mouth, the weight of his body pressing her down into the sand . . .

'Not quite like that,' she said unsteadily.

There was a moment of intense silence, broken only by the sound of water slapping against the jetty. Drew looked up at her from the boat. It might have been laughter dancing in his eyes, or it might just have been the reflection of the light on the water. A smile was curling his mouth. He remembered yesterday afternoon as well as she did. Carey stared desperately away, waiting for some scathing comment about lying again, but his smile only deepened as he turned away to start the outboard.

'Let's go,' was all he said.

CHAPTER SEVEN

CAREY watched the white sand shelving away beneath them as the little boat nosed its way out across the lagoon. The water was so clear that she could see right down to the fish darting in and out of the turtle weed that swayed in the limpid depths. Drew anchored among the clumps of coral that formed the shallow inner barrier of the reef, where they were still protected by the still waters of the lagoon, and when he shut off the engine the silence seemed to envelop them.

'At the risk of having my head bitten off, I'd suggest you make sure that the backs of your legs and arms are well covered in cream,' he said, tossing across a much squeezed tube of sunblock.

Carey caught it automatically. 'Surely it's not necessary at this time of day?' she said, and glanced around them. The temperature was perfect and the air had a softness and a freshness it lost later in the day when the heat built up into a harsh glare.

'It is for you,' said Drew in a tone that brooked no argument. 'You're not used to the sun out here, and there's no point in trying to put some on later when you're wet.' His eyes slid appreciatively down the long, slender length of her bare legs. 'You don't want to spoil that lovely skin of yours, do you?'

Carey pressed her lips together and unscrewed the top of the sunblock. Drew adjusted the straps on a pair of flippers while she stood up and self-consciously slathered the cream over her arms and legs. He watched her critically with his light eyes and when she had finished ordered her to turn round.

'I thought so,' he said as she turned awkwardly. The waves breaking over the reef rocked the boat from side to side before rippling on and subsiding into the still lagoon, and Carey staggered slightly, instinctively reaching out for his shoulders to keep her balance. Drew steadied her with hard hands on her hips and when the wave had passed turned her impersonally so that she faced away from him. 'You've missed the backs of your thighs,' he told her. 'There's no point in just slapping a bit behind your knees and hoping for the best. Here, give me the cream.'

Rather sullenly, Carey passed it down to him and he squeezed some on to his palm. Still holding her firmly, he rubbed it over the backs of her thighs. His hands were hard, slightly calloused, very sure as they smoothed over her skin. Carey bit down hard on her lip, but when he reached the tender flesh at the line of her swimsuit she gasped and stepped away so sharply that the boat rocked alarmingly and she nearly lost her balance.

'I can do that myself!'

'Don't be ridiculous!' snapped Drew, pulling her back without ceremony. 'Those are the very bits that get most burnt, and it's impossible to see for yourself. Believe me, if you want to be able to sit down for the rest of your stay, you'd better put up with it, distasteful as my touch obviously is to you!'

Carey's face was burning by the time he had finished, although Drew himself was unmoved by the intimacy of his task. 'Try these on for size,' he said, passing up a pair of flippers.

'I've never snorkelled before,' said Carey, trying to sound as briskly practical as he did. 'What do I have to do?'

'Just float,' he said, pulling on his mask and snorkel to hang round his neck. 'The mask will protect your eyes and you can breathe easily through the snorkel in your mouth. The flippers give you added buoyancy, and of course make it much easier to swim.' Drew had on his own flippers and leant forward to check Carey's. 'They seem OK. Not too loose?'

She shook her head, and he went on, 'Now, the main thing is to stay close to me, and whatever you do don't touch anything. There are sea-urchins everywhere and their spines can be very painful. So can some of the sponges, and the coral's much sharper than it looks, so be careful. Keep away from jellyfish, too. Don't stick your hand down any cracks either, or you're liable to get a nasty bite from a moray eel that will make you jump away a lot faster than you do from me!'

Carey flushed and set her teeth. She was beginning to feel rather less enthusiastic about the idea of going snorkelling. She hadn't realised there were quite so many hidden dangers lurking in these limpid waters.

'And another thing,' said Drew, struck by another thought. 'If you get tired, don't be tempted to rest on a shelf. Quite apart from the fact that you might damage the coral, you won't see a scorpion fish until it stings you. A sting-ray won't be very happy if you step on it either, but they usually stick to the sandy bottom, and although you're in the shallows here you'll be way out of your depth and won't be able to stand up anyway. Still, it's as well to be aware of them.'

Carey peered over the edge of the boat. It didn't look very shallow to her. In fact, it looked very deep. She swallowed. 'Are there any sharks round here?'

'You get some small inshore sharks,' said Drew casually. 'They're unlikely to be interested in you, though.'

'How likely is unlikely?' Carey asked with another nervous glance at the water.

'Very unlikely. They're interested in fish, not humans, so as long as you don't flap around and panic and generally look like an appetising meal in trouble they won't bother you.'

Carey wasn't exactly reassured by his sang-froid. 'Perhaps I'll just sit in the boat after all,' she said with an assumption of nonchalance, but Drew only grinned and tossed her a mask and snorkel.

'Don't be so wet!'

He slipped into the water, hanging on to the side of the boat with one hand while Carey splashed inelegantly in beside him. The water was cooler out here and she gave an involuntary gasp, swallowing a mouthful of water which left her choking and spluttering as she flailed desperately for the boat.

Drew put out a hard hand and lifted her up so that she could cling to the side of the boat while she got her breath back. He sighed. 'I suppose you *can* swim?'

'Of course I can!'

'It doesn't look like it,' he said caustically. 'The first rule is to keep your mouth shut!'

He waited until Carey had recovered slightly, then showed her how to breathe through her snorkel and float on the surface of the water. It looked simplicity itself, but Carey kept getting water in her snorkel, which brought her upright, coughing in panic.

'For God's sake!' said Drew irritably the fourth time it happened. 'Relax!'

'How can I relax when there are hordes of sharks and sting-rays and all those other beastly things you mentioned all circling around beneath me?' she demanded snappishly.

Drew forced himself to sound patient. 'Do you think I'd be in the water if I thought there was any likelihood of a horde of circling sharks?'

'You've probably dragged me here as bait for one of your rotten experiments!' she said sulkily, and he grinned suddenly, and the sunlight bouncing off the sea caught his eyes.

'Could this be the same girl who came running down the jetty in case I came out without her?'

Carey cast him a look of loathing. 'I've changed my mind.'

'I know you'll find this hard to believe, Carey, but there isn't a single creature on this reef who has any interest in you at all... Except one, maybe,' he added judiciously, his face alight with laughter. The reflected light from the water rocked over his skin and Carey felt herself skewered by a terrible desire to smile back at him, to wrap her arms around his neck and hang in the water, held hard against his body. It was so strong that she forgot her fears in the simple need to keep breathing, slowly, in and out.

'Look, try once more,' he was saying persuasively, and Carey nodded dumbly, desperate to hide her face in the water in case he read the naked longing in her eyes. And this time it clicked. Concentrating so hard on her breathing, Carey forgot to panic, and before she knew it she was floating effortlessly along beside Drew, propelling herself with her flippers.

It was another world, just as he had said. Drew had marked out ten-metre-square transects with nylon rope and he worked his way steadily over to one where he began making notes on special underwater paper. Carey hardly noticed what he was doing. Entranced, she hung in the water, the sound of her own breathing loud and eerie in her ears as she gazed down at the silent scene beneath her. She had never imagined such colours, such weird and wonderful shapes. The corals came in a bewildering variety, some branching like antlers, others lobed obscenely like brains, rounded clumps and long fingers and wide, flat growths like tables, others so surreal that Carey didn't know *what* they looked like.

And in among it all were the fish . . . blue and green and black and yellow and purple and orange, brilliantly striped or speckled, a fashion designer's dream come true. They would swim languorously in and out of the coral until something would startle them and then they would accelerate with breathtaking speed, darting for shelter. An angel fish stared dispassionately into Carey's mask before vanishing in a flash of blue and yellow, and all around her swarmed a myriad tiny, iridescent fish, invisible until the sun caught them, transforming them into a shimmer of glinting lights.

Lost in the magical display, Carey even forgot about Drew, working methodically near by. She didn't know how long they drifted before he touched her arm and indicated that they should head back to the boat.

'That was *wonderful*!' she gasped, pulling out her snorkel as she grabbed on to the side. 'Oh, Drew, it was so beautiful!' She tugged off her mask and threw it into the boat. Her face was alight, vivid with delight as she turned to him where he hung in the water beside her.

Drops of water clung to her lashes and her eyes were silver in the sunshine, her smile warm and spontaneous.

Something flared in Drew's eyes and he took a sharp breath before turning away to drop his flippers one after the other into the boat. The muscles in his shoulders bunched and he swung himself up into the boat. Carey tried to do the same, but she wasn't strong enough and she kept falling back into the water until Drew leant over and lifted her up bodily under her arms to arrive in a crumpled, untidy heap in the bottom of the boat.

'Thank you!' Still gasping with effort, Carey clambered on to a seat and sat there panting, too delighted by what she had seen to resent her own clumsiness or Drew's rough handling.

'I'd no idea you wanted to be a marine biologist,' he remarked, amused.

She glanced at him rather shyly. 'I saw you had a copy of your book here. Could I read it?'

'Of course,' said Drew, and she sensed rather than saw that he was pleased. 'If you really want to.'

'I do,' she said. 'Now that I've seen what it can be like, I'd really like to find out more. It must be wonderful to be able to spend your whole life studying what goes on in the sea, although on second thoughts I don't know how you ever manage to do any work. I think I'd spend all day just watching it all.'

'Observation is the most important part of what we do,' said Drew, taking a pull at the water bottle, and Carey noticed that the strain had gone from his voice. 'We can't just gasp at the beauty, though. We have to note exactly what we see, so that we can build up a detailed picture of the reef and how it works. The more you know, the more fascinating it is.'

'You must know everything there is to know about this reef by now,' said Carey enviously, and Drew laughed—he really laughed.

'Hardly! The sea covers seventy per cent of the earth's surface, but if you do read my book you'll find out just how little we know about it. You could spend years studying a tiny part of it, like this reef—observing, measuring, analysing, testing hypotheses—and still be trying to understand exactly how the different systems interact.'

His laugh seemed to wrap Carey in its tingling warmth. Dragging her eyes away from his face, she busied herself finding the fruit she had brought and offered Drew a banana. He took one and she unpeeled her own, biting into it thoughtfully, considering what he had said and remembering how he had looked when he'd laughed. 'Have you always wanted to be a scientist?' she asked rather indistinctly through the banana.

'Not consciously,' said Drew, looking out across the reef to where a tiny island floated on the horizon. 'But I was the sort of little boy who always had his pockets full of beetles and earwigs, so I suppose it was inevitable.'

'I'll bet you kept tadpoles in a jamjar too!'

His gaze came back to Carey. Now that the odd moment of tension had evaporated, she had relaxed and was laughing across at him, her eyes full of sunshine. He grinned. 'Naturally!'

'We used to count the spots on ladybirds,' she said reminiscently, 'but I think that's as close to natural history as we ever came.'

'We?'

She hesitated. 'My cousin and I,' she said eventually. 'I didn't have any brothers and sisters and neither did she, so we used to spend our holidays together. We were always much closer than most of the sisters I knew.'

'Is she like you?' Drew asked, watching her idly, and, reassured by his lack of suspicion, Carey gave a mischievous smile.

'No, she's quite different. She's very glamorous, very confident, full of... what's the word?... *chutzpah*.'

'She sounds rather more like the Camilla I was expecting,' Drew commented.

Carey held her breath. She felt so relaxed and happy that she had given away more than she should have done. Would Drew guess the truth? She was torn between her loyalty to Camilla and a longing for him to know the truth, that it was not she who had had the disastrous affair with Paul Jarman. It was a longing Carey chose not to analyse too closely. She was ashamed of herself for even dreaming of something which would inevitably ruin her cousin's career, and she tried, with a sort of desperation, to change the subject before Drew began to wonder why her missing cousin resembled so much the girl he had originally been expecting.

'Did... didn't you ever think about doing anything other than research?'

'I thought about it, yes.' Drew's mouth had settled back into grim lines, as if the memory was not a happy one. 'The idea was for me to take over my father's companies when he retired. It wasn't a responsibility I particularly wanted, but I was prepared to take it on for my father's sake.'

Carey found it hard to imagine Drew in a suit, in an office, hedged in by memos and reports and appointment diaries. He was a man who belonged with a wide, empty horizon.

'What made you change your mind?' she asked curiously, and Drew's face closed as abruptly as if a shutter had dropped.

'You could say that it was changed for me,' he said in a bitter voice. 'The companies had to be sold before my father retired, so there was nothing left for me to take over.'

'I'm sorry,' she said a little awkwardly. Drew had admitted that he hadn't wanted to take over the companies, so why should he be so bitter about the fact that he had been free to carry on with what he really wanted to do? He might have resented losing what sounded like a considerable inheritance, of course, but he didn't strike Carey as a man who cared overmuch for money.

She glanced at Drew, wishing she knew just what had put that guarded look in his eyes, and wondering if she dared ask him, but before she could pluck up the courage he reached abruptly for his mask and a portable meter.

'I want to take some oxygen measurements. Do you want to have another go, or would you rather stay in the boat?'

'Oh, no, I'll come with you,' she said, speculation forgotten in her eagerness to rediscover the silent, colourful world below them.

Drew slid into the water with the economy of movement that was so typical of him and waited until Carey had lowered herself, much less elegantly, down beside him.

'You'd better stay close,' he said, adjusting his mask, and she nodded, happy to follow him further out on to the crest of the reef where the wash of waves was stronger but the corals so spectacular that Carey hardly noticed. Absorbed, enthralled, wishing that she had an underwater camera, she drifted with the current, and it was only when the depths between the coral outcrops became darker and vaguely menacing that she thought to take her head out of the water and look for Drew.

For one dreadful, heart-stopping moment, she couldn't see him and an iciness closed around her heart. Surely nothing could happen to *Drew*? Carey glanced round wildly, feeling as if she had lost her one anchor, her security. The blue sky and the glittering aquamarine water seemed to darken until, with a rush of relief so intense it was almost painful, she glimpsed his snorkel surfacing from a dive some distance away. How had she come so far?

Suddenly desperate for his reassuring presence, Carey put her head back in the water and headed resolutely back towards Drew, but the current was against her and even with her flippers she struggled to make any progress. Now the coral which had so entranced her was sinister, the fish watchful, and the obscenely wafting fingers of the sea anemones seemed to reach out and grasp for her as she swam past.

Carey's heart was pounding with effort and a vague, flickering fear, and when a huge shadow darted out in front of her she jerked upright and back against a wickedly sharp outcrop that tore through her T-shirt and scraped viciously across her shoulder. Unable to prevent a gasp of pain, Carey choked as she swallowed a mouthful of water. Coughing, horribly aware of the black depths below her and her own failing strength, Carey felt suffocating panic tighten about her, and her arms and legs flailed in a desperate attempt to find a footing. She caught hold of something, but it was the nylon rope marking the transect and the next instant it had broken free of its marker buoy and was tangling itself around her while she beat at it helplessly.

Her own terrified, choking gasps drowned out the sound of Drew's approach. When he seized her in his arms, her first reaction was to struggle in sheer panic.

'Stop that!' he ordered sharply, holding her wildly beating arms away from him, and Carey, instinctively obeying the unmistakable note of command in his voice, burst into tears and flung her arms round his neck.

'What the hell are you playing at?' Drew demanded savagely, but he let her cling to him until her hysterical sobs had died into hiccuping gasps. Easing off her mask, he let her rub her stinging, streaming eyes. 'Do you want every shark in the Caribbean to come and see what's looking so temptingly vulnerable?' He pushed her away from him slightly so that he could disentangle her from the nylon rope. 'And look what you've done to my transect!' he said furiously. 'You've ruined it! What were you doing?'

Carey could feel the white heat of his anger, but she couldn't bring herself to let him go. He was so firm, so solid, so safe. She couldn't even answer, just shook her head and clung closer. Drew controlled himself with an effort.

'I'd better get you back to the boat before you do any more damage. Can you swim, or do you want me to tow you?'

'I can s-swim,' Carey gasped, trying desperately to get herself under control. She released him reluctantly and trod water while she put on her mask.

'We'll take it gently,' he said, and stayed close beside her for what seemed to Carey an endless swim back to the boat. She was too weak even to try and haul herself into the boat, and just hung to the side, gasping for breath, until Drew could pull her in.

'*Now* would you like to explain to me what you were doing over there playing at shark bait?' he snarled. There were white lines on either side of his mouth and his eyes were light with a mixture of fury and fear. 'I *told* you to stay close to me, but did you listen? No, of course you didn't!'

'I didn't realise you weren't there,' said Carey between stiff lips, dragging herself on to a seat and letting her head hang down between her knees, limp and shaking with reaction.

'You should have——' Drew broke off abruptly. 'You're bleeding!' His voice was like a whiplash as he pushed her to one side and bent down beside to examine the blood-stained tear on her shoulder. 'What happened?'

'I don't know,' she said with difficulty. 'I thought I saw a shark and I backed into something.' She bit down hard on her lip as Drew lifted her arms and pulled the T-shirt over her head.

'Does that hurt?'

'Yes.'

'Then it's no more than you deserve,' he snapped, but his fingers were gentle against her shoulder. 'It doesn't look as bad as I thought. It's just a graze.'

'My shoulder feels as if it's on fire,' said Carey a little faintly.

'You probably scraped it against some fire coral…was it red?'

'I didn't notice,' she said, recovering enough to feel sulky at his lack of sympathy. '*I'm* not a marine biologist.'

'If you were, you might behave a little more sensibly in the water,' said Drew astringently, and moved back to pull up the anchor and start the engine.

All the way back to the jetty, Carey had to suffer a diatribe about her stupidity, her irresponsibility, her utter lack of common sense. If she had been less preoccupied with the burning sensation in her shoulder, she might have wondered if his fury had not been fanned out of all proportion by his fear for her, and she would have listened more humbly. Instead, she lost her own temper.

'All right, all *right*!' she shouted, putting her hands over her ears. 'Anyone would think I'd deliberately set out to ruin your morning!'

'You couldn't have done it more effectively if you'd tried,' he snapped back. 'I've wasted a morning's work because of you, quite apart from the time I'll have to spend repairing that transect you tore apart.'

'I haven't noticed the world coming to an end! You can't tell me a bit of rope is that important!'

'It's a damned sight more important than anything *you* do,' Drew bit out, his nostrils flaring and his mouth thin with anger. 'But of course you wouldn't agree with that, would you? You're so self-centred, you think the whole world revolves around you, and you're too shallow to realise that safeguarding the future of a fragile system like a coral reef is far, far more important than all your cynical, pretentious little plans. *Nothing* about you is important, Carey, Camilla or whatever you feel like calling yourself today! You don't achieve anything, you don't produce anything, you don't even learn anything... all you do is exploit, and don't try and tell me *that's* important!'

Tense with anger and pain, Carey stalked along the jetty and up to the hut where she managed with difficulty to peel off her swimsuit with one arm. She was struggling to tie her sarong around her when Drew marched through the bead curtain with a basin of water and a towel.

'Get out.'

'Don't be childish, Carey,' he said in a grating voice and put the bowl down on the floor so that he could straighten and retie her sarong with deft fingers.

The contemptuous intimacy of the gesture infuriated Carey even more. 'Leave me alone!'

'I'd be delighted to,' said Drew coldly. 'Believe me, I've got about as much desire to make love to you as I have to flounder around out there with the sharks, which is what you could still be doing if I hadn't come and got you, and if you don't calm down and start acting sensibly I'll take you right back and leave you to it!' He pointed to the bed. 'Lie on your front. I'm going to bathe that graze. If it gets infected, you'll be even more trouble than you are already.'

After one fulminating look, Carey did as she was told. He washed her shoulder, dried it gently with a clean towel and dusted it with antibiotic powder. 'You'd better stay here for the rest of the day,' he said curtly when he had finished. 'The burning sensation will go away eventually, but if you're sensible—and so far I've no reason to believe that you are—you'll keep it out of the sun.'

And he walked out.

Carey lay on her stomach, her fists clenched by her head, at first angry and humiliated, and then, as the day wore on, simply miserable. She had ruined everything. She remembered how happy she had been sitting on the boat with him, breathless and excited by her first glimpse of the reef. She remembered how Drew had grinned and told her about his pockets full of beetles. He had so nearly let down his guard until the memory of his father's bankruptcy had brought it clanging back into place. And then she had only made things worse by disobeying his specific instructions and stupidly panicking. Carey wanted to curl up with embarrassment when she thought about the fuss she had made. How could she have clung to him like that, sobbing hysterically, and then had the nerve to shout at Drew as if it were all *his* fault?

By four o'clock, the terrible burning in her shoulder had subsided, just as Drew had said. If she flexed her arm, she could still feel a twinge, but otherwise she felt ten times better than she had expected to only an hour before. She put on her shorts and a soft cotton shirt, rolling its sleeves up to the elbow before knotting it casually around her waist.

Pausing only to find her hat, Carey went down the steps and shaded her eyes with her hand as she looked up and down the beach. Drew was sitting on the jetty, his legs dangling in the limpid water, his fingers busy untangling a fishing line.

Carey hesitated, then headed down the beach towards him. Drew cast her one brief glance as she walked along the jetty, but said nothing. She sat down beside him, letting her legs dangle beside his, and for a while there was silence. Carey watched the way the gently rocking water distorted her feet. Drew kept his attention fixed on the tangled fishing line.

'I'm sorry,' she said eventually in a small voice, still studying the water. 'I was stupid.'

He looked up at that, a quick, keen look that seemed to go right through her, then his eyes dropped back to the knots. 'Are you feeling better?' was all he said.

'Yes. Thank you.'

Another silence fell until, inevitably, they both spoke at the same time.

'I didn't——' Carey began, just as Drew said,

'Do you——?'

They broke off with embarrassed looks. 'You go first,' said Drew.

'I just wanted to thank you,' she said in a rush, and he lifted an eyebrow in surprise.

'*Thank* me? For asking if you felt better?'

'For showing me the reef,' said Carey, looking back at their feet. Her own looked very pale next to Drew's long brown ones. 'I thought it was magical,' she went on in a low voice, and then, even lower, 'I wish I hadn't spoilt everything.'

Drew dropped the line and reached out to brush her hair aside and rest his hand on the nape of her neck. It was warm and comforting and peculiarly exciting. Carey kept staring into the water, but she was agonisingly aware of his thumb caressing the soft skin beneath her jaw almost absently, sending shivers of feeling skittering down her spine. 'And I wish I hadn't shouted at you like that,' he said. 'It's slow work without an assistant, and the group of volunteers we were expecting can't come until a month later than normal, so I'm falling behind on the research. I'm afraid I've been taking out my frustration on you, when the truth is that I shouldn't have let you drift off in the first place.' He paused. 'I'll take better care of you next time.'

Next time? Carey raised her eyes and turned to look into his eyes. They were so green, so clear, startlingly light between those thick, sooty lashes. 'You'll take me again?' she whispered, and he smiled.

'If you do as you're told.'

A slow answering smile started in Carey's eyes and spread over her face. 'I will, I promise.' The tight ball of misery that had been gathering inside her all afternoon was melting into a glow of tingling happiness. She never knew how long they sat smiling on the jetty, linked only by the warm pressure of his palm against her nape, his fingers curving around her neck, his thumb rubbing gently over her skin.

'Don't you want to know what I was going to say to you?' Drew asked at last, as if only just remembering to withdraw his hand.

Carey tried not to think how cold her neck felt without it. 'What?' She didn't know what she thought he was going to say, but it certainly wasn't the answer she was expecting.

'Do you want to come fishing?'

CHAPTER EIGHT

DREW cut the engine and the silence enveloped them, broken only by the slap of the waves against the boat. The glare of the sun was fading as it began its slow dip down towards the horizon and the sea was blue and still.

Carey watched as Drew showed her how to bait her hand-line and swing it over the side, trying to concentrate on what he was saying instead of how strong and brown his fingers were. The nape of her neck was still tingling where his hand had rested.

He had set up a proper rod at the back of the boat, clipping it into place against the rails. It left him free to squat down beside it and let another line slide through his competent hands.

'Fresh fish for supper tonight,' he said, and settled his hat down on his head as he sat back patiently to wait.

Carey rested her elbows on her knees and propped her chin in one hand. From out here beyond the reef, the cay looked still and serene. The huts were hidden in the clearing and only the rickety jetty betrayed any kind of human presence. Her eyes rested on it, remembering how they had smiled at each other. The uneven wooden planks had dug into her thighs, and the water had been cool around her feet, but she had been aware only of Drew, the light in his eyes and the whiteness of his teeth and the feel of his hand.

In the hushed light, the lagoon was a still, translucent green. As Carey watched, a breath of wind just ruffled the surface, sending tiny ripples shivering towards the beach, and a shaft of pure happiness shot through her.

It's February, she thought with an air of unreality. At home it would be dark and cold and the wind would sting her cheeks and set her teeth on edge. She would be trudging home from the shop to sit by her fire and contemplate another lonely evening. Instead she was here, sitting in a boat with the sun warm on her back. Drew was sitting beside her with the hat shadowing his face and when they had finished they would go back to the cay and have it all to themselves. There would be no one there to ask where they had been or what they had been doing or what they were going to do. They would be alone with the lagoon and the hot wind soughing through the palms.

Carey looked at the jetty and smiled.

'What are you thinking about?' asked Drew with the same odd note in his voice she had heard before. She turned back to look at him, her eyes clear and shining and her mouth still curved in a secret smile.

'I'm just happy.'

The brim shaded most of his face, but she saw something leap in his eyes. He was staring at her as if he had never seen her before. Carey looked back, and deep inside her a trembling began. She felt as if his eyes were reaching into her and squeezing her heart, tighter and tighter until she couldn't breathe.

She had forgotten the fishing line in her hand. When it jerked once, then harder, she jumped as if she had been slapped back to reality.

'I think I've caught something!'

'Pull it up,' said Drew, pulling in his own line. 'Quickly!'

'I can't. It's too heavy.' The thin plastic line was digging into her fingers and Drew came to crouch close beside her and take the weight with his strong hands. She would never have been able to bring it up without him, and it was he who flipped it over the side and put it quickly out of its wildly flapping misery.

'Good God, look at the size of it!' He burst out laughing and Carey laughed with him, her eyes sparkling with excitement.

'I thought it had to be at least a shark, the fight it was putting up,' she said. 'What is it?'

'A fat snapper, and very tasty too.' Drew dropped the fish into a bucket of water. 'Well done!'

His teeth flashed white in the shadow of his hat as he grinned up at her, and Carey felt her stomach disappear. She stared at him, stunned by the flash of blinding recognition.

'Beginner's luck,' she said in a voice that sounded quite unlike her own, but inside she was thinking, Oh, no...oh, no...no, I can't be... He was arrogant and impatient and suspicious. He was only pretending to be nice to her. The truth was that he disliked her and distrusted her and despised everything he thought she stood for. She *couldn't* be in love with him.

But she was.

Carey was quiet over supper. She hardly tasted the snapper which she had been so proud of catching and which Drew had insisted on cooking for her. Once or twice she caught him looking at her closely, and her gaze would slide quickly away. She wished he didn't have such keen eyes, and that her own weren't quite so transparent.

Most of all, she wished she didn't love him.

Wryly, Carey remembered how confidently she had told herself that she wouldn't be satisfied with anything less than a perfect love. Drew wasn't perfect; he never would be. He was nothing like the man she would have imagined for herself, but after only two days she knew with an overwhelming sense of recognition that he had become an intrinsic part of her. Without him now, she would always be somehow less than whole.

She hadn't expected love to be like this. She had had some vague, romantic idea that when the right man came along everything would fall perfectly into place, but it wasn't going to be like that. There would be no happy ending. In two weeks' time she would be gone, and Drew would be glad to see the back of her. He had made his own feelings clear enough. Even if by some miracle he came to like her for herself, it was obvious that he was too bitter about marriage ever to commit himself. There was no future for her with him.

There was no future for her without him either.

They had sat on the steps with a beer as the sun had set. Carey watched as the great fiery ball slid down below the horizon in a blaze of red and gold and knew that whatever happened she would remember that moment for the rest of her life: the stillness, the silence, the hushed, unearthly light and the sunset glow softening Drew's face. It hurt just to look at him. Carey kept her eyes fixed on the sky instead but she was excruciatingly conscious of his lean, compact strength beside her. She wanted to lean against him and run her hands over his body. She wanted to kiss her way along his jaw to his mouth. She wanted to feel his heart beating and tell him she loved him.

The words trembled on her tongue, but then the sun sank out of sight, drawing all the colour of the day down with it. It seemed to be a signal for a return of reality. Drew put down his beer, the insects began their frantic whirring, and Carey realised how near she had come to betraying herself.

How could she tell Drew she loved him when she couldn't even tell him who she was?

The meal seemed to last forever. Carey longed for it to end, but paradoxically, as soon as Drew pushed back his stool and announced that he would go out while she got ready for bed, she longed for the means to keep him near her. She stared miserably down at her hands.

'I'm sorry.'

Drew halted at the door and turned in surprise. 'What on earth for?'

'I've made things so awkward for you,' she said, unable to meet his eyes. 'You shouldn't have to hang around in the dark because of me.'

'I don't. I go down to the beach every night whether you're here or not.'

'Really?' she asked, suspecting him of being polite, and Drew gave one of his heart-shaking smiles.

'Really,' he confirmed gravely. 'Come with me if you don't believe me.'

Carey knew it was a mistake. She had every intention of smiling coolly and announcing that she was tired and would rather go to bed, but somehow she found herself getting to her feet and following Drew down the steps.

Outside, the moonlight was silver-bright. It threw shadows through the palms on to the white beach and striped a shining path across the lagoon. Drew and Carey walked slowly along the shoreline without speaking, without touching. Beneath their bare feet, the sand was cool and soft in the darkness. Carey felt as if she could feel every grain pushing up between her toes.

When Drew stopped, she stopped too. The lagoon sighed and a curve of silver water rippled quietly over her feet.

'I come down here every night,' he said, almost as if to himself. 'Sometimes I walk, but most of the time I just lie and look at the stars. We scientists like to think that given enough time and enough brain power we'll know everything, but when you look up at a night sky here the only thing you know is that we never will.'

He walked back up the beach and lay down where the sand was softer and drier, the moonshadows dappling his body, and after a moment Carey stretched out beside him. She had never seen such stars before. There were so many of them that the blue-black sky was blurry with light.

For a while they lay in silence, staring up at the stars, until Carey grew dizzy, awed by their immensity and brilliance, and certain that she could feel the earth spinning slowly beneath her. They made her feel like an insignificant speck, and she longed to be able to reach out and touch Drew's reassuringly human warmth.

'Can you recognise any of them?' she asked, more to hear his voice than anything else.

'Some of them. The brightest star in the sky is Sirius . . . see, there it is up there,' he said, pointing. 'That's part of the constellation called Canus Major— the dog—and next to that is Canus Minor. They call that Procyon, the Pup. The dogs run with the mighty hunter, Orion . . . you can spot him easily because of his belt of three stars . . . there, can you see?'

Carey followed his pointing finger. 'Yes . . . yes, I see them.' Their voices were hushed, as if they were afraid of disturbing the silence. 'Which other ones can you recognise?'

'Well, Orion and his dogs are chasing the constellation of Taurus, the Bull.' Drew leant up on one elbow to point across her. 'See that reddish star?'

Carey squinted, but shook her head. 'Where?'

'There.' Drew leant lower across her so that he could try and follow the direction of her gaze. 'Follow a line up from the end of the jetty... got it?'

'Yes!'

'That's Aldebaran,' he said. 'They call it the fiery eye of the wicked bull.'

'The fiery eye...' Carey echoed softly. 'Which...?' She trailed off as her eyes came down from the star to find Drew still leaning over her. His face was very close, the gleam of moonlight just catching his eyes and the curve of his mouth.

The question she had been going to ask dried on her lips as her breathing shortened and her pulse began to boom in her ears. She stared helplessly up at him, every sense snarled with a terrible desire to feel him and touch him and taste him.

Drew was searching her face with his eyes. 'Which...?' he prompted wickedly, well aware that Carey had forgotten about the stars, had forgotten about everything except the terrible temptation which racked her. 'What were you going to ask?'

'Which... which...?' Carey couldn't get her tongue to work. It felt thick and unwieldy and she moistened her lips. 'I can't remember,' she whispered at last, admitting defeat.

There was a long, long silence. It was Drew who broke it first.

'I'd like to kiss you,' he said, and his voice was deep and low and very warm. 'But I won't if you say you don't want me to.' He waited for Carey to absorb what he had said. 'I don't want you to say afterwards that I forced you or took advantage of you. It's time for you to be honest with me, Carey. If you want me to carry on telling you about the stars, then I will, but if you want me to kiss you then all you have to do is say so.'

Carey's eyes were huge in the moonlight. Drew was braced above her, but he wasn't touching her at all. He was making no attempt to persuade her, even though he must have known that it would have taken little more than a finger trailing down her cheek to crumble her defences.

It was up to her. A stern, sensible voice inside her warned her that she would regret it, that if she let herself get too involved it would only make it harder to leave, but Carey closed her mind to it. She might not have a future with Drew, but she could have the here and now. Deep down, she knew that she didn't really have a choice. She had never been capable of pushing him away.

Above them, the palm fronds sighed in a stir of breeze, and the lagoon whispered against the shore.

'Well?' said Drew softly. 'Have you decided?'

Carey swallowed. 'Yes.'

'Does that mean you *would* like me to kiss you?'

'Yes.'

His smile gleamed. 'I hoped that was what you would say,' he said, but he didn't kiss her immediately. Instead, he lowered himself very slowly on to her, still watching her face, and as she felt his weight settle on her Carey took a sharp breath of anticipation that wavered into confusion as still he didn't kiss her.

Smoothing the hair back from her face with his hands, he bent at last and kissed the pulse that beat below first one ear, then the other. His lips were warm and gentle, but inexpressibly exciting, and he smiled against her skin as he felt her instinctive quiver of response. Slowly, deliberately, he began to kiss his way down the curve of her cheek until, unable to wait any longer, Carey turned her face so that she could meet his kiss with a sigh of exquisite release.

She felt him shift on her and wound her arms round his neck to pull him closer as he pressed her down into the sand, his mouth more insistent now, more demanding. Carey gave herself up utterly to the sheer delight of their kisses. Drew had forced her to be honest, and this was what had been simmering at the back of her mind all day. There could be no pretence before the surge of sensation that was sucking them both up into a wild spiral of excitement. It left Carey gasping as his lips left hers at last to press a burning path down her throat while his hand slid beneath the sarong she had tied around her waist, impatiently exploring the silken length of her thigh.

Her fingers were entwined in his hair as she arched her body up to his exploration. She was electrified by his touch, afire with need, and when his mouth found hers again she kissed him back almost desperately.

Drew's roaming hands were at the buttons of her shirt, his breathing as ragged as her own. 'Do you want me to stop?' he murmured against her lips, but Carey had no hesitation this time.

'No... no... don't stop,' she breathed, tightening her arms around him.

He undid the buttons of her shirt one by one, letting his lips follow his deft fingers down, not hurrying, tormenting her senses until she arched back her head and moaned with pleasure. When the last button was undone, he brushed her shirt aside to feast his eyes on her. Her skin was pearly, luminous in the moonlight and he took a sharp breath before bending down to her once more. His hands swept back up to cup her breasts, curving possessively around them as his mouth sought their soft delight, and he murmured her name hungrily.

Carey's fingers were digging into his shoulders, almost frightened by the spinning sensations he aroused. His tongue flickered, touched, tasted, teased. She was like fire in his arms, a flame that burned higher and higher with the frantic beat of her heart, and when his mouth drifted luxuriously back up to hers she rolled over on top of him, still kissing.

Unprotesting, unashamed, she let him slide the shirt from her shoulders while she did as she had been longing to do all day and savoured the male-rough skin of his jaw, with its faint prickle of stubble. She kissed his ear, his temple, working her way down to his chin and back to his mouth while Drew smoothed his hard hands over her back, tracing the line of her spine and finding the graze on her shoulder.

'Does it hurt?' he murmured, running his fingers over it very gently, and Carey smiled into his ear.

'I can hardly feel a thing!'

All she felt was joyous, liberated. Never before had she given herself so completely to the sheer unadulterated pleasure of a man's body. It was her turn now to unbutton his shirt and let her hands drift with a shiver of desire over his sleek skin. He was like tempered steel, firm yet supple, his muscles flexing in response to her touch, his own hands moving with an increasing urgency over her curves.

Drew was unwinding her sarong. Carey kissed her way down his throat and on down that irresistible arrow of hair until she reached the waistband of his trousers. Lifting herself up on one arm, she looked down into his face, her eyes dilated with desire. The silky hair slithered forward to swing down past her cheek and she flicked it back breathlessly.

'Now it's your turn to be honest,' she said softly. 'Do *you* want to stop?'

Drew held her face tightly between his hands. 'I don't think we can, do you?' he said, and brought her down hard against him for a kiss that was fierce with passion.

It went on and on, charged with a rocketing excitement, so that Carey murmured in disappointed protest when he pulled his mouth reluctantly away to discard the rest of their clothes with swift, sure hands and spread out her sarong. Swinging Carey back beneath him, Drew paused to stare deep into her eyes, and then, at last, the time for hesitation was past. He was right. There was no way they could stop now.

Carey gasped at the thrilling explosion of sensation as he covered her and their bodies met unimpeded for the first time. Their hands moved with a new urgency and their kisses were deep with a shared longing that bore them on and up together to where nothing existed but the throb of need and the hard heat of Drew's body. Carey drew a long, shuddering breath as it claimed her at last, engulfing them both in a swirling tide of feeling. It swept them along in a timeless, instinctive rhythm, and she sobbed his name, terrified that he would leave her with this aching need that only he could fulfil.

But Drew didn't leave her. He took her with him, and together they hesitated on the very brink, before plunging into an ecstatic dive that left them crying out to each other through a whirl of wonder and fulfilment.

Later, much later, they went down to the still lagoon and sank into its cool, silken water. Carey was preternaturally aware of it lapping seductively against her tingling skin. The stars seemed even brighter than they were before, so bright that she wondered if this was all just a dream and she would wake at home in Yorkshire with the rain rattling against the window.

Then Drew swam over to her and she slid wordlessly into his arms and knew that it wasn't a dream. It was real, wonderfully real. As they kissed, the moonshine slipped over them and shimmered out to the horizon.

'You're beautiful,' said Drew, kissing her shoulder. 'But then I'm not the first poor fool to tell you that, am I?'

The bitterness lacing his voice made Carey flinch as the *real* reality hit her. He still thought she was Camilla, had thought she was Camilla all the time he was making love to her.

'Drew, I——' She broke off, appalled at how badly she wanted to break her promise to Camilla. But would it make any difference? He would still feel that she had deceived him. Carey buried her face in his throat, breathing in the salt on his skin with a kind of desperation. It was ironic that it was the very honesty which kept her from making promises lightly that kept him so distrustful of her. But she *had* promised and, for Carey, a promise once made couldn't be broken.

She lifted her head and looked into his eyes. 'I can't make you trust me, Drew. I think you must know how special what just happened between us was for me, but, if you don't believe me, nothing I can say is going to change your mind.'

Drew's hands were sliding up and down her arms half reluctantly, as if he resented the fact that he couldn't stop touching her. 'I don't know what to think any more,' he said after a moment. 'I've seen too much pain caused by dishonest women to forget it all because of a moment's madness in the moonlight.'

'You mean you don't want to forget,' said Carey despairingly.

'I *can't* forget,' he corrected her. 'That doesn't mean we can't carry on as we did before and pretend there's no past, and no future, just the next two weeks, just as you suggested. Let's be realistic. We both know where we stand; we both know that when the two weeks are up you'll be leaving. We don't have to make any promises or try to persuade each other of anything. We can just make the most of the present.'

Carey was silent. Her heart cracked at the coolness in Drew's voice, but she knew that he was right. She would have to leave. Why should they waste the time they had together trying to change what had gone before? They had now.

It was all they had.

There was no point in wishing that he loved her enough to forget everything else. He didn't. He might not be able to promise her a lifetime of happiness, but he was offering her two weeks. Carey thought of the heart-stopping rapture he had shown her, and knew that she would take whatever he had to give. If two weeks was all she could have, it would have to be enough.

Drew's hands had stilled on her shoulders as he waited for her reply. 'I think you're right,' she said at last, lifting her eyes to his. 'I'm prepared to be realistic if you are. Let's just make the most of the time we have together.'

She felt Drew relax. 'And how shall we do that?' he murmured and pulled her slowly towards him.

Carey leant against him, putting her arms around his wonderfully solid body and pressing her mouth to the pulse that beat at the base of his throat. 'What about the same way we made the most of tonight?' she suggested, a smile quivering on her lips, and Drew's deliciously drifting hands closed hard about her.

'So you think we should spend the next two weeks making love?'

'We-ll...'

'Do I take it that you want me to carry you out and start again right now?' he asked wickedly.

Carey feigned indignation. 'I didn't say that——' she began, breaking off with a gasp as Drew swept her up into his arms and waded back towards the beach.

'Because that's what I'm going to do,' he said, and did.

Drew was gone when Carey woke the next morning. It was very late, and the room was hot and airless, but she lay watching the way the bright light slanted through the open door and fell in irregular stripes through the bead curtain, thinking about the night before, about Drew and the intoxicating passion they had found together. Carey had discovered feelings that she wouldn't have been able even to imagine before, a joy so complete that she knew she would never be the same again. No matter what happened now, she would always be grateful to Drew for that.

Drew... the memory of his hard body rippled over her skin. Carey stretched, feeling the unfamiliar stiffness of her muscles, and sat up slowly. Two weeks, they had agreed last night. It had been easy to agree in the darkness, washed by the silver moonlight, but would it be the same in the bright light of day?

Carey felt unaccountably shy as she dressed and went in search of Drew. He had obviously just got back from the reef, for he was tying the boat up to the jetty and his hair was wet. He straightened as Carey walked towards him, watching her approach with intensely light eyes that made her heart lurch uncomfortably. It was impossible to tell what he was thinking. He just stood there and waited for her.

What if he regretted making love to her? What if he resented her for breaking through his guard, or despised her for succumbing so easily?

Carey faltered, suddenly awkward. Why couldn't she be blasé like Camilla? She wished she hadn't come. She should have let *him* come to find *her*. 'Hello,' she said a little breathlessly and then, ridiculously, she blushed.

The unreadable look in Drew's eyes dissolved into amusement. 'Why, Carey!' he said, with that unmistakable undercurrent of laughter in his voice. 'I didn't know girls like you still blushed!'

Rigid with humiliation, furious with herself, with him, Carey made as if to turn away, but he reached out and caught her by the hand. Lifting it, he twisted it to press a warm kiss where the blue vein pulsed in her wrist. When he glanced up from it, Carey saw that he was smiling, and her own embarrassment faded into a glow of happiness. Drew felt her relax as he dropped light, tantalising kisses along the soft skin of her inner arm to her elbow, and then on to the warm curve of her shoulder before pulling her, unresisting, towards him.

'Hello,' he said at last, and kissed her.

For Carey, the next ten days were a time out of time, an enchanted idyll in a real-life paradise where she and Drew were alone with the sea and the sky and the stars. Looking back, she was amazed at how quickly they fell into a routine. Without it ever being discussed, she began to act as his assistant. She spent long hours floating still on her stomach recording indecipherable signals, or reading off levels of light and oxygen and salinity. She learnt how to map transects, to bait and trap fish, to tag the captures and then track them, and was able to put her own skills to use with Drew's underwater camera, waiting patiently for the perfect shot. Much of the work was tedious and repetitive, but Carey didn't mind. If Drew had let her, she would have spent all day in the warm water, spellbound by the silent world beneath her and happy in the knowledge that Drew was close beside her.

They would work together companionably in the mornings until Carey broke off to go and prepare some lunch. Remembering what Drew had told her about his usual diet, she made it a point of honour never to resort to the tins of tuna that were stacked up in the storeroom. He would have plenty of fish when she had gone. Carey deliberately tried to keep reminding herself that the enchantment would end, but it was hard to believe when Drew was there, smiling at her, holding her, kissing her. Sometimes she made herself think of the hours ticking away relentlessly, but it only made her more desperate to make the most of the time she had.

She would look at Drew, at the sun glancing off the water, at the fringed shadows the palm leaves cast on the sand, and think with a kind of panic, I must remember this. She treasured the way the boat rocked gently in the swell, the way Drew screwed up his eyes against the light, hoarding memories of the marbled light wavering in the shallows and the ever-present sound of the sea surging against the reef and the smell of the wooden floorboards and the feel of the sand beneath her as Drew laid her down and bent to kiss her.

He taught her to dive, too, and showed her the extraordinary richness of the reef. Carey loved to listen to him talk about the complex marine world and as she began to recognise the fish with their strange names—needle fish, butterfly fish, angel fish, damselfish, trumpetfish, cowfish, goatfish... the list went on and on—she became more and more fascinated with the reef. Drew could spot the most cleverly camouflaged creature; he would touch her arm and point and Carey could only marvel that he had seen it at all. He talked about how little they really knew of the sea, but to Carey his knowledge seemed inexhaustible. When he was not in the sea, he would be working on his solar-powered lap-top computer, his expression absorbed. Carey envied him his ability to concentrate utterly on what he was doing. She had been reading his book, enjoying the spare economy of his prose and the wit and elegance of his descriptions, but, no matter how fascinated she was, her eyes still kept drifting back to Drew. Even floating through the magic of the reef, there was always a part of her that was aware only of him, of his smile and his mouth and his lean brown body.

When work was finished for the day, they would walk around the island, or sit on the jetty waiting for the sunset, or take the boat out and fish for their supper. Carey never repeated her first great success, but she liked just sitting in the boat and watching Drew, unaware of the way she glowed with happiness. Her skin had acquired a golden bloom, and her brown hair was streaked with sunshine. Sometimes Drew would glance up and their eyes would meet and they would smile, each knowing that the other was thinking of the night before and the night that was to come...

And they talked. They argued and laughed and exchanged views on everything except the things that mattered most to them. Carey couldn't tell him about

Camilla or her life in Yorkshire—although several times she nearly slipped up—and Drew never mentioned his family or why he was so suspicious of women. It cost Carey everything not to tell him how much she loved him, but they both stuck scrupulously to the agreement they had made.

They wouldn't consider the past or the future, but think only of the present, and when Drew took her hand every night and led her down the steps through the moonshadows Carey told herself that it was enough.

CHAPTER NINE

THE idyll lasted ten days.

It was Carey who spoilt it. Afterwards, she wondered if things would have been different if she had kept quiet, but at the time all she could think about was the fact that there were only two more days before she was due to leave, and she felt compelled to try and give Drew some hint of why she had acted as she had so that later, when he found out the truth, as he inevitably would one day, he might remember and understand.

They were lying on the beach in the starlight, still tangled together after a lovemaking which had left them both shaken with its plenitude. They would never be closer than this, Carey thought, and her fingers drifted hesitantly over his broad shoulders, loving the feel of the sleek skin over those steely muscles.

'Drew?'

'Mmm?' he said lazily, sweeping one hand in luxurious possession over her slender curves.

'Which do you think is more important, honesty or loyalty?'

His hand stilled and he lifted himself up slightly to look at her. 'Why?'

'I just wanted to know what you thought.'

'You know what I think,' said Drew. Abruptly he moved away from her and sat up, frowning, and Carey levered herself up beside him.

'I know what you think about honesty. I don't know what you think about loyalty.'

'They go together, surely?' he said a little impatiently. 'How can you be loyal to someone unless you're honest with them?'

'What about if someone else is involved?'

Carey thought that it was a strong hint, but to her dismay Drew completely misinterpreted it. 'If you're about to confess some other affair, I don't want to hear about it,' he said almost violently. 'I'm not interested in what you do when you leave here.' His eyes narrowed as Carey winced. 'What's the matter? Is that *too* honest for you?'

She looked away from him to the starlight glimmering on the lagoon. 'You're not telling me anything I didn't already know,' she said in a low voice.

'Isn't it better that way?' he demanded harshly. 'Look what kind of mess we'd be in now if I'd pretended to be in love with you! Believe me, I know enough of the misery *that* kind of dishonesty can cause. To have any chance of success, a relationship has to be utterly honest right from the start.' His voice was very bitter. 'Pretence and secrets just destroy it from within.'

'Is that what happened to you?' Carey asked, amazed at how even her voice could sound when inside her heart was lacerated with pain.

'It happens to everybody,' said Drew flatly. 'It happened to Paul, it happened to my father, and yes, it happened to me, too.'

He rested his arms on his raised knees and stared out to where the waves breaking over the reef just caught the glimmer of moonlight. For a long time, he said nothing, and when he did Carey thought at first that he had changed the subject completely. 'My father was a very wealthy man,' he said, almost conversationally. 'People used to think he had everything—success, influence, a loving wife and family—and then everything went wrong. My mother died about twenty years ago. He grieved for her, but, like many people, he found his solace in work, and the company expanded even further. And then, five years later, he married again.'

A grim note had come into his voice and Carey glanced at him. 'Five years is a long time to be on your own,' she said neutrally. 'He must have been lonely.'

'Oh, I understand why he wanted to get married,' said Drew. 'What I can't understand is why he wanted to marry Kelly. He was an intelligent man, intelligent enough to build up a business empire and make millions, but he couldn't see that Kelly was taking him for a ride.' He shook his head as if remembering how baffled he had been. '*She* was clever... no, not clever, *cunning*. She'd worked out exactly how to appeal to a lonely old man. A rich lonely old man. She pretended to be sweet and demure and helpless, and of course he fell for it. It was an irresistible combination, particularly in a girl as lovely as Kelly. Who wouldn't be flattered at having the full battery of her charms turned on him?' he asked bitterly.

Carey cast him another sideways glance. Had Kelly turned her charms on Drew, too? Was that why he was so bitter? 'You didn't like her?'

'I hated her,' he said simply. 'She destroyed my father. She played him like an expert until the ring was firmly on her finger, and then she set out to use him and deceive him. It took him about a year to realise what she was doing, and when he did he was devastated. He was a very proud man. He would have given her the world, but she turned their marriage into something cheap and nasty and sordid!'

'What did she say when he told her he knew she was deceiving him?'

'She lied,' said Drew. 'She lied and lied and lied some more. My father struggled through another couple of years, and then even he couldn't make any more excuses for her. She'd run through his capital by then, so she didn't even bother lying any more. Instead she took him to the cleaners for a quiet divorce. He had to sell up the last of his companies.' Drew paused and his mouth twisted. 'He was never the same after that. He'd worked all his life to build up his empire, and he'd planned to pass it on to me. It broke his heart to admit that he'd thrown it all away on a worthless little tramp. God knows, I didn't care about the money, but I did care about him. It was terrible to see such a proud, vigorous man broken like that. He died two years ago. I think he couldn't bear to go on living with the humiliation any longer.' His expression twisted again. 'And the worst thing is, I was just as much a fool as he was.'

Carey sat up straighter. 'You don't mean you and Kelly...?'

'Kelly?' Drew sounded incredulous. 'No, I recognised Kelly for what she was right from the start. I wasn't quite so clever about my own fiancée, though,' he added bitterly.

'Fiancée?' Carey echoed in a hollow voice. 'I thought you'd never got married.'

'I haven't. It was the only good thing that came out of the whole sorry mess. If it hadn't been for Kelly, I'd have married Danielle.' His expression was distant, remembering.

'What happened?' asked Carey hesitantly.

'Kelly happened. When I first met Danielle, I was the heir to a business empire. I was young, too, or perhaps

I would have realised that those innocent looks disguised a heart quite as avaricious as Kelly's. Fool that I was, I really believed Danielle when she said that she loved me, but all she really loved was the Tarrant fortune. When that went, Danielle went too,' he said in a flat, deliberately expressionless voice. 'All in all, I think I had a lucky escape. I ended up free to do the research I wanted, which I certainly wouldn't have been able to do saddled with a grasping wife, even if Danielle had been prepared to face life as the wife of an impoverished scientist. It wasn't easy, but I had some grants, and since *Beneath the Blue* money hasn't been a problem. I doubt if Danielle would have thought it worth her while to hang around all those years in between, though.'

Drew's mouth was set in a bleak line. 'I'm glad now that I discovered exactly what she was in time. Now I've got a secure financial background for my research without having to waste any of it keeping some demanding wife. After all, it was Danielle who taught me not to trust women. If it hadn't been for her, I might have fallen for some other pretty face and be working in a city somewhere, struggling to support a wife and several squalling children. Instead of which, I'm here, and I'm free.' He glanced around him. 'I ought to feel grateful to her. Yes,' he went on thoughtfully. 'I think I was lucky. Very lucky.'

Carey suspected that he hadn't thought so at the time. The young Drew would have been desperately hurt, already reeling from the blow of his father's humiliation. 'I'm sorry,' she said uncomfortably, wishing she could think of something more adequate to say. 'I see now why you feel so strongly about dishonesty, but that was just two women. We're not all like Kelly and Danielle.'

'Perhaps women don't all go to their extremes, but in my experience they're all dishonest to some degree.'

'Drew, that's not fair!'

'Isn't it?' he demanded angrily. 'Can you put your hand on your heart and tell me that you never lie?'

She longed to tell him the truth, but the ties of loyalty and affection that bound her to Camilla were too strong to break. If he had loved her, she would have had to tell him, but he didn't. He wouldn't let himself love anyone. All he cared about was his independence, having the freedom to carry on his research. He could hardly have made it clearer that he had no intention of ever being tied down by the demands of a wife and family. 'I'm not interested in what you do when you leave here,' he had said.

A flush rose in her cheeks. 'No,' she said miserably. 'I can't.'

'I didn't think you could,' he sneered. 'You've been giving a very fine performance, Carey, but I haven't forgotten what you really are.'

Carey whitened. 'Haven't these last days meant anything to you?'

'No more than they have to you,' he said in a cold, hard voice that cut into her heart. 'I suppose you thought I'd be like Paul, so besotted with your lovely body that I'd forget everything else I knew about you, but you can't make a fool out of me. It's been a very pleasant two weeks, but let's not pretend that it's meant anything to either of us. That wasn't in the deal.'

'No, it wasn't, was it?' said Carey very softly. She felt numb as she got to her feet and shook the sand from her sarong.

Drew looked up at her sharply. 'Where are you going?'

'I'm rather tired.' She wrapped the sarong around her with unsteady fingers. 'I think I'll go in.'

Inside, she was as cold as ice. She lay on her bed and let the truth beat at her. Those magical days had meant nothing to Drew. Nothing.

Nothing. Nothing. *Nothing*.

'To have any chance of success, a relationship has to be utterly honest right from the start.' He was right, she realised wearily. She hadn't been honest with him, and, even if she confessed the truth now, there would always be the memory of deception between them.

Well, what had she expected? Had she really thought that Drew would come to love her in spite of everything? It was time to stop dreaming and come down to earth. The magic was over, and now she had to face the future.

Drew came in much later. He hesitated just inside the curtain. 'Carey?' he said very softly.

Carey didn't answer. She closed her eyes and pretended to be asleep, and in the darkness he couldn't see the tears pouring down her cheeks.

The next morning, she was pleasant but withdrawn. Drew cast a penetrating look at her strained face as he handed her a mug of tea, but he made no comment. Breakfast was usually a quiet meal, but warmed by a smile of shared memory, or Drew's hand sliding down her hair in a light caress. Today the silence was dead and cold and they avoided looking at each other at all.

'Are you ready?' said Drew when they had finished. He was standing by the door, putting on his hat, and his voice sounded harsh in the tense atmosphere.

Carey would have given anything to go with him, to work beside him and know that she could reach out and touch him when she wanted, that at any minute he might turn and smile at her. But it would only make things harder in the end.

'I think I'd better do some notes today,' she said, amazed at her own coolness. 'I've only got today and tomorrow and I haven't done anything I came to do yet. I need to take some photographs, too.'

Drew's nostrils looked pinched. 'You've been taking photographs all week!'

'Not the sort of photographs Weatherill Willis will be interested in.'

His expression hardened at the calculated reminder of her priorities. 'You mean suitable sites for a hotel?'

'That kind of thing,' she agreed evenly.

'Far be it from me to keep you from such important work,' he said savagely. A muscle beat furiously in his cheek. 'Will you be able to spare a moment for lunch?'

'I'll probably take something with me,' said Carey, pretending not to notice his sarcasm. 'You carry on without me.'

'That shouldn't be too difficult!' Drew snapped and turned on his heel to stride down the steps.

Left alone, Carey found that her fingers were clenched around the handle of her mug. Her knuckles were white with the effort of self-control. Drearily, she tidied up the hut and packed herself some bananas and a bottle of water.

She spent the day on the far side of the island. The very thought of building a resort in this magical spot made her shudder, but she had to have some excuse to be by herself. She concentrated on making a note of all the difficulties that would be involved in building in a place like this, in the faint hope that she might be able to persuade Camilla to put in a discouraging report after all.

Carey ate the bananas in the lonely shade of a leaning palm. She missed Drew with a physical ache. Yesterday, they had lain in the shade together after lunch. She had closed her eyes and pretended to sleep until Drew's hands drifting tantalisingly over her body had coaxed her into a slow, luxurious smile, as he must have known they would, and she had reached up to draw him down to her...

The memory was so vivid that Carey gasped as if she had been lanced with pain. If it was like this now, what was it going to be like when she was back in Yorkshire? She pressed her hands to her eyes. How was she going to bear it?

She would have to bear it.

Carey straightened her back. As the long day passed, she found that anger was the best relief for the black, desperate misery that threatened to engulf her. It didn't cure it, it didn't make it go away, but it made it easier to pretend. She let herself get angry with herself as well as with Drew. She blamed herself furiously for falling in love so hopelessly, for giving herself up so heedlessly to the enchantment of their time together when she'd known that she would have to face reality eventually. And she blamed Drew for his stubbornness and obtuseness. How could he possibly think that the last two weeks hadn't meant anything to her? He must be stupidly blind not to realise how much she loved him. Hadn't he learnt *anything* about her?

Apparently not, Carey thought bitterly. He preferred to stick to his prejudices. It ought to be obvious that she wasn't the kind of girl who had indulged in a disastrous affair with Paul Jarman. Surely he could see that she wasn't anything like Kelly or Danielle, but did it occur to Drew Tarrant that he might—just once!—be wrong?

Of course it didn't! He was too pigheaded and arrogant! If he were half as clever as he thought he was, he would have guessed at once that she wasn't Camilla. He should have *forced* her to tell the truth, instead of letting her fall in love with him. Was it her fault that he was too stubborn and stupid to work things out for himself?

So Carey stayed away all day, stoking the comforting burn of anger, and her temper was still afire in self-defence as she made her way back to the hut. The sun was just sinking into the sea and Drew was pacing tensely on the veranda as she slipped through the trees into the clearing.

'Where the hell have you been?' he snarled, springing down the steps to catch her by the arms and shake her in fury.

She wrenched herself from his grasp. 'On the other side.'

'All day?'

'I had a lot to do,' she said coldly.

Drew's mouth was thin with temper. 'I don't suppose it occurred to you that I might be worrying about where you were?'

Carey lifted her chin and met his blazing eyes with a flash of defiance. 'I was under the impression that you wouldn't care very much either way!'

'Who said anything about caring?' Drew had recovered quickly from a tiny pause. 'The only thing I was worrying about was whether I was going to have to tramp around in the darkness looking for you.'

'Well, you haven't had to, have you?' Carey brushed past him rudely and stamped up the steps. 'Contrary to what you seem to think, I can survive perfectly well without you.'

'Oh, I don't doubt that for a moment,' he sneered.
'Girls like you are only too capable of looking after
themselves.'

Supper was very tense. They spoke to each other only
when absolutely essential, while suppressed rage boiled
in the silence between them. Afterwards, Carey went out
to wash, determined to go straight to bed, but Drew was
waiting for her at the bottom of the steps.

'Are you planning to do more of your famous research tomorrow?'

'I expect so,' she said frigidly.

'I find it hard to believe that it takes two whole days
to realise that a cay like this is totally unsuitable for development. Five minutes ought to have been enough!'

Carey set her teeth. 'I'm here to collect the facts. It's
not my decision to make.'

'And you're offering that as a sop of your conscience,
are you? What about all you had to say about the reef?
You told me you thought it was magical, that it ought
to be preserved at all costs, or have you changed your
mind about that too?'

'No!'

'Then how can you even *consider* putting forward in-
formation that might lead to its destruction?'

'I've got a job to do,' Carey said stonily.

'Oh, your *job*!' Drew's voice was icy with contempt.
'Now we get to the truth of the matter! Did you really
think you could make me believe that the time we've
spent together has meant anything to you? All you care
about is yourself. And money. And ambition. You'll do
anything to make sure you get your own way, won't you?
You were determined to come here and you were going
to stay even if it meant seducing me!'

Carey's face was white, her fists clenched. 'Now who's not being honest?' she spat furiously. 'You're the one who's so keen on the *facts*, Mr High and Mighty Scientist, and the fact was that *you* seduced *me*!'

'Is that how it seemed to you?' Drew demanded bitterly. 'And I suppose the way you looked at me with those big grey eyes of yours had nothing to do with it? The way you walked towards me and smiled? The way your skin quivered whenever I touched you——?' He broke off and tried to master his rage, his jaw working furiously. 'Oh, it was very cleverly done, Carey, and I fell for it hook, line and sinker! Don't try and tell me you didn't seduce me!'

'Why would I want to?' she shouted, too angry to think clearly. 'Have you ever thought about that? Did it ever occur to you to wonder why I've spent two weeks putting up with your arrogance? Of course not! You never thought about me as a person at all. You made up your mind about me before you even met me, and nothing was going to change your mind. You didn't care that I might have my own reasons for being here, reasons that were important to me. No, the only thing you think is important is your rotten project!'

Carey's eyes were glittering with fury. 'You're a fine one to accuse me of being self-centred, when all you think about is your precious research! And then you have the nerve to accuse me of seducing you! Why don't you tell it like it really happened, Drew? You're so obsessed with the reef that you were prepared to do anything to make sure you could carry on with your work undisturbed, and that meant making sure I didn't do mine, even if it meant making love to me . . . a rather crude way of keeping my mind off the job, wasn't it?'

'It worked, didn't it?' said Drew callously.

'Yes, it nearly did.' Her voice was shaking with suppressed emotion. She wouldn't cry in front of him. She *wouldn't*! 'Nearly, but not quite. I realised in time just how pompous and selfish and pigheaded you really are! I'm sick of listening to you criticising me for something you know nothing about. I'm sick of being held responsible for the crimes of every woman who ever existed. I'm sick of *you*! You think you're so clever, don't you? But you're too stupid to see the truth when it's right in front of your nose!'

She made to push past him again, but Drew grabbed her arm and swung her back. 'What do you mean by that?'

'You're the scientist,' said Carey in freezing accents. 'You've done all the research you need.' Shaking her arm free, she stalked up the steps, turning when she reached the veranda to look down to where Drew was glaring up at her, the moonlight slanting through the trees just catching one side of his face. 'Work it out for yourself!'

Drew had gone when Carey woke the next morning. His camp bed didn't look as if it had been slept in at all, but the kettle was warm, so he had obviously been in.

Tomorrow she would have to leave. This is my last day here, Carey kept repeating to herself, but the words just circled in her head meaninglessly. It was impossible to imagine a day when she wouldn't wake with the sunlight chinking through the bamboo and the sound of the lagoon washing lazily against the beach, a day when she would watch the sun rise up to the glare of midday and then sink slowly, slowly into the sea once more.

For want of anything else to do, Carey cleared up the hut, so crushed with misery that she found herself moving stiffly like an old woman. Afterwards, she sat on the veranda, staring blindly out across the lagoon. Immersed in her own black thoughts, she didn't notice the boat approaching until it was almost at the jetty. It was the first visitor they had had for two weeks.

The last thing Carey wanted to do was to make polite conversation, but she could hardly ignore the boat. Drew might be anywhere. Reluctantly, she walked across to the edge of the clearing, stopping in relief when she saw that Drew was there after all. He was leaning down from the jetty, taking a packet of letters from Francis. Carey recognised him from the day she had arrived; it seemed a lifetime ago now. He had evidently just come to drop off the post and a crate of fresh vegetables, for he didn't even bother switching off his engine, merely handing everything up to Drew then raising a hand in a casual farewell before heading the boat back out to the gap in the reef.

Drew was glancing casually through the letters. The handwriting on one made him stiffen in surprise, but he dropped them into the crate so that he could pick it up and carry it with two free hands.

Seeing that he was heading for the hut, Carey retreated hastily. She couldn't face Drew yet. Without pausing to collect her hat or any water, she slipped through the trees and along the path to the far side of the cay.

It was thirst that drove her back in the end. She made her way cautiously into the clearing, but Drew had had plenty of time to read his letters and go back to whatever he had been doing before Francis arrived. Carey calculated that she had plenty of time to fetch some fruit and water and escape back to her solitary beach before Drew came back in search of lunch. They had parted on such bitter terms last night that the less she saw of him the better now.

The contrast between the dazzling midday light outside and the cool shade of the hut was so great that Carey hesitated in the doorway, blinking as her eyes adjusted to the gloom. When they did, her heart almost stopped, for Drew was sitting, grim and silent, at the table, a letter spread out in front of him.

'I've been waiting for you,' he said in a voice that set apprehension clawing at her spine.

'Oh?' Carey's throat was even drier than it had been before and she poured herself some water from the bottle that stood on the side, turning her back so that Drew wouldn't see that her hands were shaking.

'Sit down, *Camilla*.'

Carey stiffened, but obeyed. She set the mug of water very carefully in front of her on the table. 'What is it?'

'You don't like me calling you Camilla, do you?' There was a menacing undercurrent to his words, and Carey hid her unsteady hands beneath the table.

'No...no, I don't.'

'But you answer to it, I see.'

She swallowed. 'What's this about?'

'It's about the fact that you've lied to me from start to finish,' said Drew, throwing her passport contemptuously on the table between them. 'A pity I didn't think to look at this before, but then you knew I wouldn't, didn't you, Miss Carey Louise Cavendish?'

'You had no right to go through my things!' said Carey angrily, snatching up her passport.

'And you had no right to come here and pretend to be someone you weren't.' The implacably icy control in Drew's voice was more frightening than if he had shouted and screamed. Every word cut Carey to the quick. 'You don't like being called Camilla because it's not your name. It's not a first name, or a second name, or a business name. It's not your name at all. Camilla Cavendish is someone completely different.'

Carey sat very still. 'How did you find out?' she asked very quietly.

'Francis brought the post this morning.' Drew's face was rigid but she knew that he was angrier than he had ever been before. 'There was a letter from Paul among the others. He was due back here next week, but he wants to stay in England a little longer as there's something he wants to do.'

'I—I don't understand,' she said, biting her lip.

'Neither did I at first. I couldn't understand why he was apologising for abandoning the project so needlessly when Camilla had clearly decided not to come after all.'

Carey took a deep breath. 'He saw Camilla?' she said dully.

'Got it in one,' said Drew, and the anger began to crack the ice in his voice. 'Paul, it seems, went up to Yorkshire to visit some friends. They took him round to see the countryside, and who should he see going into one of the shops but the very girl who'd haunted his dreams for so long. Paul tells me it was quite a revelation. He had run away from here because he was afraid of meeting her again and it had all been for nothing. Apparently he's decided it's time he faced up to the past. He couldn't talk to Camilla with his hosts there, so he's going back up to Yorkshire on his own this week. He thought I'd like to know that he's going to get her out of his system once and for all,' Drew finished with biting irony. He looked across the table with glacial green eyes. 'Well? Would you like to tell me who you really are?'

'I'm Camilla's cousin,' she said, quailing inwardly at his expression but paradoxically relieved that the deception was over at last.

'And everything you've told me since you arrived has been a lie?'

'I lied to you about being Camilla, that's all.'

'That's *all*?' Drew repeated furiously, the icy control dissolving abruptly in a blaze of rage. 'You come out here, pretend to be someone you're not and make a complete and utter fool of me, and you think *that's all*! No wonder you accused me of being stupid last night! You must have had a good laugh over the last two weeks!'

Carey linked her hands together to stop them shaking. 'Did it seem to you as if I was laughing at you, Drew?' she asked quietly. 'I wanted to tell you who I was, but I promised Camilla that I wouldn't.'

'Why did you do it, Carey?' Suddenly Drew sounded very tired.

'I did it for Camilla,' she said. 'She's desperate to get ahead in her job, and presenting a development plan for Moonshadow Cay seemed the only way she could get her foot in the door, as it were. She was going to come herself, but she broke her ankle, and she didn't trust any of her colleagues to give her the credit if they came in her place. So she asked me to come. We didn't think it would matter which Miss Cavendish you got.' Carey hesitated, looked down at her hands. 'It was only when I got here and met you that I realised it did matter.'

'You could have told me,' he said flatly, bitterly.

'No, I couldn't. I promised Camilla.'

'And her career was more important than the time we spent here together?'

How could she make him understand? 'She's the only family I've got,' said Carey. 'People think she's spoilt and ambitious, but she's always been there whenever I needed her. I couldn't let her down.' Lifting her head, she looked squarely into his angry green eyes, her own direct and steely grey. 'And after all you made it very clear that what we had together meant nothing to you. Why *should* I have told you? You were determined to distrust me whatever I did.'

Drew's expression was closed and granite-hard. 'How right I was!' he said savagely. 'It's ironic that I was on my way to find you when Francis arrived. And do you know what I was going to tell you?'

'No,' she whispered.

'I was going to tell you that I'd been awake all night, thinking about what you'd said. I was going to tell you that I'd been remembering the time we shared and how clear your eyes were, and that I'd let myself believe that I'd been mistaken in you. I actually allowed myself to think that you were different and that I might be able to trust you after all.' He gave a bitter laugh. 'That should keep you and Camilla in fits!'

Carey looked at him bleakly. 'I don't think it's very funny.'

'Neither do I,' said Drew, and it was as if a shutter had come down over his eyes. 'You've proved that I was right about women all along, Carey. You so nearly had me convinced, against all the evidence, that I was wrong, but you turned out to be as dishonest as all the rest.' The stool scraped across the floor as he pushed it back and stood up. 'You needn't bother staring up at me with those innocent eyes of yours. I might have fallen for them once, but I won't make the same mistake again. Now get your things. I'm taking you to Belize City right now, and you can find your own way to the airport tomorrow. I can manage without Weatherill Willis's sponsorship as long as it means I don't ever have to see you or hear from you again!'

CHAPTER TEN

LATER, all Carey could remember of that silent journey back to Belize City was thinking numbly what a beautiful day it was, so different from the day she had arrived. Today the sea glittered calmly beneath a glorious blue sky, and the sun beat down on Carey's shoulders, but she was far more miserable than she had been when she'd huddled beneath the plastic bags with the rain pouring down her neck.

Drew didn't bother to turn off the engine as he brought the boat up against the jetty at Haulover Creek. He hadn't said a word since that last dreadful scene in the hut. He slung her suitcase up on to the pier and stood grimly holding the boat steady so that she could climb out.

This was it. Carey's mind cracked in panic as she realised that she would never see Drew again. He was waiting for her to get out of the boat and walk out of his life.

'Drew,' she said desperately, not knowing what she could say, knowing only that she couldn't leave like this; but his face was completely closed.

'Get out.'

Silently, Carey handed up her camera-bag and clambered out on to the jetty. Drew jumped down into the boat, reversed it back out into the creek and pointed the bow out to sea once more. Slamming on the throttle, the boat seemed to leap forward and skim over the water as he headed out to sea without a backward look.

Carey never knew how she got herself home. She spent that night in a dilapidated guest house, lying on the bed, afraid to move in case she shattered with pain. Somehow she must have got herself to the airport and changed planes at Miami, but all she remembered was Drew, the sea and the sky and the stir of the breeze in the palms and the fact that he hadn't come to the airport to stop her getting on the plane and flying away.

She arrived back in Yorkshire on a beautifully crisp day. The frost glittered on the grass and the sky was a pale winter blue. It was the sort of day Carey had once loved, but after the vivid colours of the Caribbean it looked only dreary and cold.

There was no sign of Camilla at the cottage, so she left her suitcase and walked down to the shop. She had fully expected her cousin to hang a 'closed' sign on the door and amuse herself for two weeks, but Camilla was not only there but looking astonishingly at home as she ushered out a bemused-looking couple who were clutching two pictures.

'Carey!' she cried in delight, spotting her cousin. She waved a final goodbye to the couple and drew Carey into the shop, muttering out of the side of her mouth, 'They were "just looking", but I managed to flog those two dreary water-colours and a tablecloth!' She gestured largely round the shop. 'Well? What do you think?'

'You've rearranged everything,' said Carey, looking round her in surprise. 'It looks much better.' It did. Her own displays had always been artistic, but Camilla's had real flair. 'You've been busy.'

Camilla gave her a proper welcoming hug. 'I've had a wonderful time,' she announced. 'I thought I'd be bored stiff stuck here for two weeks, but I've never enjoyed myself so much before! Everyone's been so kind and friendly. I don't know how I'm going to face going back to London.' She hesitated and glanced sideways at Carey. 'In fact, I'm thinking of resigning from Weatherill Willis and buying a shop up here like you.'

Carey's jaw dropped. 'But I thought you were desperate to become a globe-trotting executive?'

'I thought I was, but I've had a lot of time to think up here and I've changed my mind.' She chattered on as she put the kettle on to boil in the little room at the back of the shop, where they could see if anyone came in.

Carey sank down in one of the comfortable chairs. 'So I needn't have gone to Belize after all?' she said in an odd voice.

'Well, if you hadn't gone, I'd never have come here and found out what I really wanted to do,' Camilla pointed out reasonably, pouring the tea. 'So it all worked out for the best.'

Carey said nothing, but she took the cup and saucer her cousin handed her. She had always liked her tea out of these delicate china cups, but now memory stirred queerly and she saw instead Drew handing her one of the battered enamel mugs... With a sharp intake of breath, she forced her eyes back into focus.

'Anyway, Carey, how are you?' Camilla was saying. She eyed her almost enviously. 'I must say you look fantastic! A tan obviously suits you, and your hair's come up beautifully in the sun. In fact,' she went on thoughtfully, 'you look quite different. I can't quite put my finger on it...'

'Did Paul Jarman come and see you?' Carey asked, breaking into this train of thought.

'Yes! Wasn't it an amazing coincidence that he should have been working on the island I was interested in?'

'Amazing,' she echoed a little drearily.

'I couldn't believe it when he walked in,' Camilla continued, cheerfully oblivious. 'Apparently he'd seen me quite by chance and tracked me down. We had a good chat about old times, though I had no idea our little fling had meant so much to him. He told me he'd been very bitter, but when he saw me he realised that in blaming me he'd just been making excuses for himself.'

'Did you know that he was engaged when he met you?' Carey asked carefully.

'*No*!' To her relief, Camilla's surprise was unmistakably genuine. 'I *thought* he was a bit shifty at times! It's just as well he wasn't on the cay when you arrived, wasn't it? He'd have rumbled you immediately! Of course, I told Paul that you'd gone instead of me, but he said he'd explain it all to Drew Tarrant when he got back.'

'He won't need to,' said Carey bleakly. 'He already knows.'

'Goodness, what did he say when he found out?'

'Quite a lot.' Carey's careful smile went a little awry, and Camilla's lovely eyes narrowed in sudden suspicion.

'Oh, Carey, I'm sorry. Did I drop you in it?'

Carey took a rather shaky breath. 'Well, let's say it was an experience.'

The door tinkled and a customer came into the shop. With a mutter of impatience, Camilla got up, but fortunately he only wanted a card, and she practically pushed him out of the door so that she could rush back to Carey.

'Tell me *all* about it,' she commanded dramatically, throwing herself down in the other chair.

Carey looked down into her cup. How could she tell Camilla about the moonshadows on the sand or the way the sunlight threw wavering reflections over Drew's skin? How could she tell her about Drew's hard hands against her body, his mouth against her breast? Her throat felt very tight. 'It was a beautiful island,' she said at last.

'I told you it would be,' said Camilla triumphantly. She leant forward. 'Was it awkward being there alone with Drew Tarrant?'

'No... not awkward.'

Her cousin looked at her with a hint of impatience. 'Well? You're being very cagey, Carey! Come on, I want to know what he was like!'

A vision of Drew rose before Carey: settling his hat on his head, turning his head to look at her, his eyes so startlingly light and green between his dark, dark lashes, drawing her down on to the sand, smiling his slow smile against her skin...

'He was... he was...' She found that she couldn't go on. Her cup rattled in its saucer as she put it down unsteadily. She tried to smile, but it simply fell apart and her mouth worked convulsively.

'Carey!' cried Camilla, horrified. She had never seen her cool, sensible cousin like this before. 'What's the matter?'

'Nothing,' said Carey, and burst into tears.

Camilla got up and took the cup and saucer from her nerveless hand. Then she turned the sign on the shop door firmly to 'closed', and passed Carey a box of tissues.

'I think you'd better tell me everything.'

Slowly, haltingly, the whole story came out. Camilla listened in growing remorse. 'It's all my fault,' she said contritely. 'I feel awful. I was having such a wonderful time here that I never gave a thought to what it might be like for you if anyone knew you were an imposter.

And now you're miserable and I can't bear seeing you cry!'

'It's not your fault,' said Carey. She heaved the jagged sigh that came at the end of a long bout of crying and scrubbed her wet cheeks with yet another tissue. 'You weren't to know that anyone there would know anything about you. It's not your fault that Drew feels so strongly about dishonesty, or that Paul didn't tell you he was engaged. It's not your fault that I fell in love with Drew either. I knew I'd have to leave, I *knew* there was no future in it, but I...I couldn't help it.'

Her voice cracked again and Camilla put a comforting arm around her shoulders. 'You don't think there's any chance that Drew might be in love with you?'

Carey shook her head miserably. 'He despises me.'

'No, he despises *me*,' Camilla corrected her kindly. 'And anyway, it doesn't sound to me as if he was acting like a man who despised you. You don't make love to someone you despise.'

'If he didn't before, he does now.' Carey's voice was muffled in a tissue. 'He'll never forgive me for deceiving him like that. Never.'

'Oh, Carey!' Camilla was almost in tears herself. 'I feel so responsible. I know quite well that it is my fault for insisting that you take my place. I just wish there were something I could do to make things better.'

'There is.' Carey screwed up the tissue into a damp ball and wiped her eyes. 'Are you serious about giving up your job with Weatherill Willis?'

'Absolutely.'

'Then put in a report discouraging them from developing a resort on Moonshadow Cay. At least then I'll know that Drew will be able to carry on with his research and something good will have come out of this mess. I'll write it tomorrow and develop the photos, and you can take everything back with you.'

So Camilla stayed in the shop while Carey sat at her kitchen table and wrote a report describing the cay and the studies Drew was carrying out on the reef and calling on Weatherill Willis to forget the idea of a resort and invest instead in creating a conservation area.

Camilla's brows rose as she read it. 'This is powerful stuff! They might even buy it.' She gasped when she saw the photos Carey had developed. 'Carey, these are fantastic!'

Carey could hardly bear to look at them. She hurt whenever she thought about the cay. The lagoon would still be there, slapping gently against the jetty, the coconut palms would still be leaning out over the beach. In the distance, the sea would be murmuring against the reef, and the hot breeze would stir the drooping fronds above the little hut. And Drew would still be there. Was he lying on the sand looking up at the stars alone? Was he thinking about her, remembering how they had made love, or was he simply glad to be rid of her?

She gave most of the photos to Camilla to take back to London, but one she kept. She had been anxious to finish a film one day, and had snapped one of Drew through the zoom. Unaware of the camera, he was standing on the jetty, looking out to the reef. Absorbed in thought, his eyes were narrowed against the glare, and his hands were thrust into the pockets of his trousers. He was wearing the same shirt he had worn the night they had first made love. Carey could remember the feel of the buttons beneath her fingers.

The cottage was very quiet when Camilla had left. Carey forced herself down to the shop every day, but she felt detached from everything, as if she had left some essential part of herself on Moonshadow Cay. She missed the light and the colours. Yorkshire in late February seemed to consist only of shades of black and white and grey. Sometimes Carey would look out of the kitchen window and instead of the frost-covered lawn leading down to the grey stone wall she would see the lagoon, shimmering in shades of turquoise and jade beneath a blue, blue sky.

The week seemed to last forever, and on the Sunday Carey took herself for a long walk in the dales. The cold stung her cheeks, but the wildness of the empty hills made her feel really alive for the first time since she had come back from Belize.

The time had come to make a break, she decided. She would never forget Drew and the cay where she had known such intense happiness, but she would have to accept that they were part of the past. Camilla had been right when she'd said that going to Belize would change her life. Perhaps things hadn't worked out quite as she had envisaged, but change it had.

She couldn't go on living here, thinking about what might have been, Carey realised. Even since her mother's death last year, she had been drifting, carrying on with the shop out of a sense of duty more than anything else, but Moonshadow Cay had given her a taste of the wider world waiting out there. If Camilla was serious about wanting the shop, she would sell it to her and concentrate on photography. Her pictures had been well-received locally, but she would never know if she could make a go of it professionally until she tried. Carey decided that she would take her camera and travel, and perhaps in time she would see so many other wonderful places that the memory of one tiny moonlit island would begin to fade.

Camilla was enthusiastic about the idea of taking over the shop. 'But I'll need to give Weatherill Willis a month's notice,' she warned. 'Can you hang on until then?'

Carey said that she could, but getting through every day was an effort. She ate little, and when she slept her dreams were all of a lean brown man with sure hands and a mouth that dissolved her bones with longing.

Two long weeks passed. It was strange how the same time had gone so quickly on the island whereas now every day seemed like a year. Carey shut the shop with relief on Friday evening and trudged home to the cottage that didn't feel like home any more.

It was cold and dark when she let herself in. She lit the fire and crouched in front of it, watching the flames flicker and take hold and remembering when the sand had been too hot to walk on. It had been a relief to sit in the shade then, to share a simple lunch while the sun hammered down around them. They had had two hours every day, adrift in their circle of shade, two hours when Drew would smile and tug her down beside him...

The doorbell rang, shrilling through her memories, and Carey realised that silent tears were pouring down her face. She wiped them away but stayed huddled in front of the fire, hoping that whoever it was would go away. She didn't want to see anyone, but the bell rang again insistently. They must have seen the tell-tale wreath of smoke curling out of the chimney.

With a sigh, Carey got up, rubbing her face with the back of her hands and switching off the hall light to try and hide the fact that she had been crying. Taking a deep, steadying breath, she opened the door.

Drew stood there.

Carey's heart stopped. The instinctive, blinding leap of joy was overwhelmed almost immediately by the conviction that her dreams were playing tricks on her, and she squeezed her eyes shut, terribly afraid that she had only imagined him and that she would find that it was only Giles or the vicar or the man across the road who was always running out of milk.

Steeling herself for the reality, she opened her eyes again, but Drew was still there. He looked strangely unlike himself in a thick black jumper, but the clever face, with its distinct angles and the irresistibly intriguing line of his mouth, was just the same.

'Drew?' she whispered incredulously as her heart slammed back into life.

'Yes.' Drew cleared his throat. His expression was tense and, incredibly, anxious. 'Can I come in?'

Carey felt as if the world had turned inside out. 'I . . . yes . . .' She trailed off, still half convinced that she was dreaming, and stood back to hold open the door. Closing it after him, she leant back against it for support. Drew's massive frame seemed to fill the narrow hallway.

They looked at each other in silence. Carey drank in the sight of him hungrily. If this was a dream, she would make the most of it before she woke in her cold, lonely bed. 'I've never seen you in a jumper before,' she said inanely, and amusement softened the tense set of Drew's mouth.

'There's not a lot of call for jumpers on Moonshadow Cay, is there?'

'No.' The cold cottage hallway faded as the memory of the cay vibrated between them, crumbling at last Carey's sense of numbed disbelief. 'What are you doing here?'

'I wanted to see you,' said Drew quietly. 'I wanted to say that I was sorry. I was so angry and disappointed when I found out that you hadn't trusted me enough to tell me who you were that I lost my head completely. I said an awful lot of things I didn't mean, Carey.'

Slowly, she straightened from the door. 'It's all right,' she said. 'I understand.'

'Do you?' Drew never took his eyes from her face. His voice was deep and low. 'Do you understand what it's been like since you left? Do you understand what it is to want someone with every fibre of your being and to know that life holds nothing unless you can hold them in your arms again? To realise that you might have lost your only chance of happiness?'

Carey's eyes glimmered with tears. 'Yes, I do understand,' she said waveringly. 'I understand exactly.' She didn't remember Drew moving, but the next instant she was in his arms and he was crushing her against him, his face buried in her soft hair while she clung to him with a kind of desperation.

It was too soon to kiss. For now they just needed to hold each other and allow themselves to believe that the hurting was over. Carey pressed her face into Drew's throat, breathing in the distinctively clean, masculine scent of him, her arms wrapped tightly around his back as if to absorb his solid strength.

'I didn't think I'd ever see you again,' she said very quietly, when she could.

'I know.' Drew's voice was muffled against her hair. 'I was foul to you. When I left you on the jetty at Haulover Creek I thought I never *wanted* to see you again. I was so angry I couldn't even see straight, but as soon as I got back to the cay I realised what I'd done. It was so empty without you. I thought I could go back to the way I was before. I told myself that I was well rid of you, that everything would be the same, but it wasn't. Nothing was the same without you.' His arms tightened ever closer around her. 'I'd got so used to your being there. I kept looking round, expecting to see you standing there, smiling, with the sun in your eyes.'

Lifting his head at last, Drew took her face between his hands, wiping away the tears that had spilled over with tender thumbs. 'I missed you, Carey,' he said simply. 'I didn't know how much I loved you until you were gone.'

Carey tried to smile but she was too happy, and the tears kept welling up and sparkling on her lashes. 'I knew how much I loved you long before then,' she said, amazed to see unmistakable relief blaze in his eyes. Then Drew took a sharp breath and surprise melted into joy at last as he bent his head and kissed her, and she forgot everything except the inexpressible delight of his mouth and the feel of his arms about her and the wonderful, glorious, rapturous knowledge that he loved her.

She remembered much later, when they had finally made it to the welcoming warmth of the sitting-room and she was curled in his lap on the sofa. 'Surely you knew I loved you?' she said, kissing his throat.

Drew smiled and slid his hand caressingly down her hair. 'I hoped you did, but I wasn't sure. For a long time I wasn't sure about *anything* as far as you were concerned. You puzzled me right from the start. I was expecting a hard-boiled sophisticate and then you walked towards me looking uncomfortable in your smart suit. You had such clear eyes, I couldn't believe that you were the dishonest Camilla I'd heard so much about, but you admitted it quite coolly. I should have guessed when you insisted that I call you Carey, but it simply never occurred to me that you weren't who you said you were, and I decided that you were just clever.

'Looking back, I can see that I was just as pigheaded and stupid as you said I was, but at the time I was thoroughly confused. I knew, or I thought I knew, that you were the girl who had treated Paul so badly, and my experience with Danielle had taught me to be very wary of girls who looked innocent but behaved quite differently. I was determined not to be made a fool of like that again. But as the days went by it was harder and harder for me to remember that. There were so many things about you that didn't add up to the image of the cold, calculating woman Paul had told me about. You were too warm, too loving, too natural. Your eyes were too frank, your smile too beautiful.' He stroked her face, holding her hard against him, and Carey wrapped her arms around his neck and smiled the smile he remembered. 'I didn't know where I was!' he confessed with a grin. 'All I knew was that I wanted you more than I've ever wanted a woman before. I kept reminding myself about Paul, telling myself that I'd live to regret getting involved with you, but I couldn't help myself, and those two weeks we had together were . . . well, you know what they were like.'

'Yes,' said Carey softly, remembering. 'I know.'

'I was ready to throw caution to the winds and ask you to stay when you asked me whether I thought honesty was more important than loyalty. I know now why you did, and of course I should have realised what you were getting at, but *then* it seemed only as if you'd thrown a bucket of cold water in my face, reminding me about Paul and my father and all the things I thought you were.'

He had pulled off his jumper in the heat of the room, and Carey laid her hand over his shirt, feeling his heart beat beneath her palm. 'You told me that that time hadn't meant anything to you,' she reminded him.

'Of course I did. I was feeling a fool for having fallen in love with you in spite of everything I knew, and I was determined you shouldn't find out just how successful you'd been in changing my mind against all the odds. I told myself I'd just been a challenge for you, and I was too proud to admit that you'd won. But it didn't stop me missing you when you withdrew the next day. I was frantic when you didn't come back to the hut, and when you *did* come you were so cool that I lost my temper and took all my frustrations out on you. It was only that night when I'd calmed down enough to think about what you'd said that I decided I could trust what *I* knew of you, not what I'd heard from Paul.

'His letter was a terrible shock; just when I'd decided that you were as honest as you'd been with me, I found out that you'd been lying to me all along...' Drew paused. 'I was furious with you for making such a fool of me, and even more furious with myself for letting you do it.'

Carey's eyes were very serious as they looked into his. 'I didn't think you would ever forgive me for deceiving you. I wanted to be honest with you, Drew.' Her voice cracked slightly. 'I'm so sorry I wasn't.'

'Don't be,' he smiled, stroking her hair. 'If you hadn't pretended to be Camilla, I'd never have met you and I'd never have found the girl I'd been waiting for for so long. You taught me to trust again, Carey, and you taught me how to love,' he said, tipping back her face, and he kissed her again.

It was a long, long time before Carey could draw a shuddering breath of happiness. 'How did you find me?'

'Oh, that was easy. The worst part was waiting for Paul to come back and take over the project. He told me all about his meeting with Camilla and how he'd realised that he'd been doing her an injustice all these years . . . but you know that, don't you?'

'Camilla can be a little thoughtless sometimes, but she really isn't cruel,' said Carey. 'She honestly didn't know that Paul was engaged when she met him.'

'Yes, she told me.'

'She *told* you? When?'

'How do you think I found you? I went straight to Weatherill Willis as soon as I got to London this morning and stormed into Camilla's office. I was furious with her for putting you in such a difficult position and planned to tell her exactly what I thought of her as soon as I'd wrung your address out of her.'

'Oh, dear,' said Carey faintly.

'You needn't worry!' he said, amused. 'Camilla is well able to take care of herself, as you must know! She'd obviously decided that attack was the best form of defence, because she tore a strip off me for treating you so badly. She told me that you were so transparently honest that I must have been blind as well as stupid not to realise immediately that you weren't her—all of which was perfectly true, so I couldn't really argue back.' Drew hesitated, held Carey closer. 'Then she told me I'd broken your heart. It's not broken, is it, Carey?'

Carey leant her head against his shoulder and sighed happily. 'Not any more.' A thought struck her. 'I wonder why she didn't ring and tell me you were coming?'

'I asked her not to. I'd been so unpleasant to you that I was afraid that if you knew I was coming you'd decide that you'd be better off without me. I wouldn't have blamed you if you'd slammed the door in my face!'

'Didn't Camilla tell you that I'd have given anything just to see you again?'

'She probably thought it would do me good to come in a humble frame of mind,' said Drew with a grin. 'One thing she *did* tell me, though, when we'd both calmed down a bit…apparently the directors of Weatherill Willis were so impressed with the report you wrote that they've decided to buy the island from Emory Jones as planned, but instead of a resort they'll protect it as a conservation area so that we can continue our research.'

Carey's eyes were like stars. 'Oh, Drew, that's *wonderful* news! So the project's safe?'

'Thanks to you, yes,' said Drew. 'There is one problem, though.'

She sat up in concern. 'What?'

'Paul wants to pursue his own line of research back here. Apparently he met up with his old fiancée when he came back, and they've decided to get engaged again.'

'That's good news, isn't it?'

'Ah, yes, but it leaves me without an assistant.'

'What are you going to do?' said Carey a little doubtfully, and Drew's eyes lit with laughter.

'Well, money's always a problem on scientific projects, as you know, so I thought the best thing I could do was get married and train my wife to be my new assistant.'

A smile quivered on Carey's lips. 'That sounds like a good idea,' she said demurely. 'Much cheaper than paying another scientist.'

'Exactly. Of course, it's not easy to find someone suitable,' said Drew thoughtfully, although his hands were sliding distractingly down her spine.

'What sort of qualities are you looking for?' she asked a little breathlessly.

'Well, I'm a very hard man to please, as you know. I need someone intelligent and trustworthy, naturally. She needs to be clean and tidy and a good cook.'

'I see,' said Carey.

'And then, of course, she has to love me to distraction and be prepared to put up with a sandy beach instead of a comfortable double bed.'

She pretended to consider. 'That doesn't sound like *too* much of a problem. I suppose she'll need to be able to swim, too?'

'Of course,' said Drew, then his smile faded. 'But most of all I need a girl with clear grey eyes and warm kisses and the truest smile in the world.' He pulled her back against him. 'I don't suppose you know of anyone suitable?' he murmured.

Carey slid her arms round his neck and kissed the corner of his mouth where a smile was tugging irresistibly. 'It just so happens that I know the perfect candidate!'

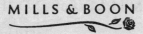

Especially
for you
on
Mother's Day

**Four new romances for just £5.99—
that's over 20% off the normal retail price!**

We're sure you'll love this year's Mother's Day Gift Pack—
four great romances all about families and children.

The Dating Game · Sandra Field
Bachelor's Family · Jessica Steele
Family Secret · Leigh Michaels
A Summer Kind of Love · Shannon Waverly

Available: February 1995   Price: £5.99

MILLS & BOON

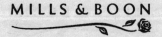

*Available from WH Smith, John Menzies, Volume One, Forbuoys,
Martins, Woolworths, Tesco, Asda, Safeway and other paperback stockists.*

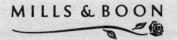

Next Month's Romances

Each month you can choose from a wide variety of romance with Mills & Boon. Below are the new titles to look out for next month, why not ask either Mills & Boon Reader Service or your Newsagent to reserve you a copy of the titles you want to buy – just tick the titles you would like and either post to Reader Service or take it to any Newsagent and ask them to order your books.

Please save me the following titles:

	Please tick	✓
BURNING WITH PASSION	*Emma Darcy*	
THE WRONG KIND OF WIFE	*Roberta Leigh*	
RAW SILK	*Anne Mather*	
ONE NIGHT OF LOVE	*Sally Wentworth*	
THUNDER ON THE REEF	*Sara Craven*	
INVITATION TO LOVE	*Leigh Michaels*	
VENGEFUL BRIDE	*Rosalie Ash*	
DARK OASIS	*Helen Brooks*	
YESTERDAY'S HUSBAND	*Angela Devine*	
TAINTED LOVE	*Alison Fraser*	
NO PLACE FOR LOVE	*Susanne McCarthy*	
THAT DEVIL LOVE	*Lee Wilkinson*	
SHINING THROUGH	*Barbara McMahon*	
MANDATE FOR MARRIAGE	*Catherine O'Connor*	
DESERT MAGIC	*Mons Daveson*	
DANGEROUS FLIRTATION	*Liz Fielding*	

If you would like to order these books in addition to your regular subscription from Mills & Boon Reader Service please send £1.90 per title to: Mills & Boon Reader Service, Freepost, P.O. Box 236, Croydon, Surrey, CR9 9EL, quote your Subscriber No:................................... (if applicable) and complete the name and address details below. Alternatively, these books are available from many local Newsagents including W H Smith, J Menzies, Martins and other paperback stockists from 10 February 1995.

Name:..

Address:...

................................Post Code:........................

To Retailer: If you would like to stock M&B books please contact your regular book/magazine wholesaler for details.